DINNER, DRINKS AND MURDER

A Food & Wine Club Mystery Book 2

CAT CHANDLER

Five Sisters Publishing

Cover Art: Carrie@cheekycovers.com

Content/Editing: Behest Indie Author Services

❊ Created with Vellum

For Mom— my greatest cheerleader to follow my dream and write books

CHAPTER ONE

"IN THE END, WHAT WE DISCOVERED WAS THAT THE CLUES WERE there for us to follow. The hard part was realizing that something we'd seen or heard was also a clue to the killer's identity."

Applause broke out around the room. Nicki beamed at her audience before turning to give her two best friends, Jenna and Alex, a wink.

"Unless it's just screaming 'I'm a clue' at you," Frances Wilder's voice was loud enough to carry over the clapping hands. She thumped her cane on the floor to emphasize her point. The oldest member of the group at ninety-five, she was also the most outspoken, and one of Nicki's favorite people. The down-to-earth Frances made no secret of the fact that at her age, she'd earned the right to speak her mind.

Maxie Edwards, the hostess for the gathering as well as the president of the Ladies in Writing Society, raised a perfectly arched brow at her long-time friend. "Oh? Just which clue do you think was screaming out, Frances?"

"The lab report, of course. Anyone could see that." Frances lifted her cane and pointed it at the dark-haired, poised and confident Alex who was sitting beside Nicki. "And a good thing there was a doctor right there to know what all those words and numbers meant."

From the corner of her eye, Nicki saw Alex's mouth curve into what her friends always called her "polite doctor smile", something Alex insisted every physician had to perfect at some point in their training. Jenna had even begun keeping a list of what she'd labeled the "secret doctor classes" that she was sure Alex had taken in medical school, which besides the "Smile Politely" entry, also included "How to Write Anything and Everything So No One Else Can Read It". Nicki loved the list. And although she stuck to expressing outrage at such a ridiculous notion as "secret doctor classes", Nicki knew that Alex was amused by Jenna's list too.

"Well, ladies, I think our fearless member, Nicki Connors, along with her two friends, Jenna and Alex, did a wonderful job of discovering the truth about George Lancer's murder," Maxie announced. "Don't you?"

Her comment led to another round of enthusiastic applause, and even Frances joined in as she smiled and nodded at the three women sitting at the head table set up on Maxie's back patio. The surrounding garden was a burst of color and beauty, a testament to the master gardener who tended to it, who was also Maxie's husband, Mason Edwards, a retired police chief.

"As a well-known food and wine writer, and the writer of a wonderful series of spy novels, Nicki is of course a prominent member of our society." Maxie went on while Nicki fought not to roll her eyes. Pronouncing her as a "well-known writer", and "prominent member" of the Society, was bit of a stretch as far as Nicki was concerned.

"Now, of course our Nicki already has a purple hat and quill." Maxie touched her own hat with a highly polished fingernail as every head in the audience bobbed their heads in agreement. And every one of them was wearing that very same, deep-purple hat with an attached quill made from a lavender colored feather. "But I would like to move to extend an honorary membership to both Jenna Lindstrom and Alex Kolman."

Nicki poked Jenna in her side when the self-proclaimed computer geek groaned out loud. Luckily the sound was drowned out by another round of enthusiastic applause. When Maxie held out hats to Alex and Jenna, they both exchanged a glance before staring at Nicki. She caught their message easily enough.

"Burgers and zucchini fries for our next lunch together if you'll put on the hats." It was Nicki's standard bribe for her friends. Alex nodded and carefully settled the purple Robin Hood style hat, with its feathery quill sticking up from the brim, onto her head. Jenna, however, continued to stare at her friend.

"Fine," Nicki said. "I won't forget the homemade ketchup with sriracha sauce."

"And the hand cut fries with sea salt for me, plus the garlic sautéed vegetables for Alex," Jenna whispered back.

Nicki shot her a skeptical look. "That's a lot to expect just to wear a hat for a few minutes."

"A hat that will instantly turn me into some kind of mutant Santa's elf."

Tall, thin, with a mop of long, dark, tightly curled hair, and brown eyes looking out from behind the lenses of oversized glasses, Jenna was right in claiming she was going to look ridiculous wearing that too-small-for-her-height hat.

The hat will probably get lost in all that hair, so all we'll see is a giant lavender feather sticking out of Jenna's head. Nicki grinned at the mental image and nodded. "French fries and vegetables it is. Now, put the thing on."

Jenna sighed and plopped the hat on her head. There were smiles and calls of congratulations from the group of ladies sitting at the tastefully decorated tables scattered all around the patio.

Alex leaned over and smiled at Jenna. "You look great, and thanks for throwing in those vegetables for me."

"I'm glad you're a better doctor than you are a negotiator," Jenna relented enough in her annoyance to smile and wave at their audience.

Maxie rose and came to stand behind Nicki's chair. She put her arms around Jenna's and Alex's shoulders as she leaned in between them. She smiled as Chloe Johnson, the historian for the Society, snapped pictures with her iPhone, and whispered, "I hope you both know that I expect you to share in that bounty from Nicki's kitchen. We're so fortunate to have such a highly trained gourmet chef among us."

Jenna turned her head and frowned at her hostess. "Why should we share? They're *your* hats."

"Oh good heavens, dear. You can't believe I would pick out such a thing. It was voted on by the entire group." Maxie kept her voice low. "They were enthralled with the idea, and there wasn't a thing I could do to stop them. Of course, as president, I did explain it was proper that I should vote only in case of a tie. Fortunately there was no need, so I didn't have to go on record as having given my approval of such a fashion challenge." She straightened and nodded at Chloe. "I'm sure that's more than enough pictures, dear. Shall we get on with the mix and mingle part of our meeting?"

For the next half-hour Nicki juggled questions about the murder she and her friends had recently solved, with equally enthusiastic inquiries about the soon-to-be-released exploit of Tyrone Blackstone, the very hunky, and completely imaginary, super-spy hero of her novels. She'd finally managed to find a quiet spot to take a breath when Suzanne Abbott and Catherine Dunton walked up and effectively trapped her in the corner.

Suzanne, who'd been dedicating herself for the last two years to becoming the best cook in the entire Society, constantly badgered Nicki for tips and advice. Her inseparable friend, Catherine, was a financial advisor who persistently tried to persuade anyone she thought had name recognition to sign on as one of her clients. For those reasons alone, Nicki tended to do her best to avoid them. But today it seemed she was out of luck.

Putting on her politest smile, and steeling herself for at least ten minutes of deflecting questions and a sales pitch, Nicki held out her hand in greeting.

"Hello, Suzanne." She shook the woman's hand and turned to her constant companion. "Catherine. How are you?"

"Busy." Catherine smiled. "Now that the divorce is final, at last, I can concentrate on my new business venture." She gave Nicki an apologetic look. "I won't be able to take on any new clients for a while. I'm very sorry."

"Oh, that's all right." Nicki had to respect the way Catherine had made it sound as if Nicki had been begging to become one of her clients. "I completely understand." She sent the pretty, middle-aged woman with the frosted blond a genuinely sympathetic smile. "Rebuilding your life after a divorce can't be easy. If there's anything I can do to help, please let me know."

Catherine's gray eyes opened wider and she blinked several times before she finally nodded. "Thank you. That's a very kind offer." She gave Nicki a wink. "Let me know the next time you're going to bring that handsome boyfriend into Mario's, and I'll be sure you have the best table in the house."

Now it was Nicki who blinked. Mario's was one of the better restaurants off the central square in the nearby town of Soldoff. Picturesque, and known for its many food, wine and art festivals, Soldoff boasted a very unusual mix of building styles around its central square, which featured a ten-foot-high, bronze statue of wine grapes. The small town acquired its name from one of its more prominent citizens who, during a trip back East, had tried to sell all the town plots that were already owned by his neighbors. Set in the heart of the Northern California wine country, Soldoff was a quiet wine-tasting stop for tourists who were on their way to the better-known town of Sonoma, located another fifteen minutes down the road.

But along with the wine tasting rooms run by most of the local wineries, Mario's Italian cuisine also drew in tourists and the locals alike. Nicki had been there often since she'd moved to the area over two years ago. She enjoyed both the food and chatting with the restaurant's owner, Mario Vincenzio.

"Rob and I do go to Mario's whenever he's in town," Nicki said. "Is Mario a client of yours?"

"A partner." Catherine's voice was tinged with pride. "I've invested in his restaurant."

"Oh?" Nicki looked over at Suzanne who nodded her confirmation. "I didn't know Mario was looking for investors."

"Just one, and I'm it." Catherine lifted her hands in a "ta-dah" gesture.

"That's great." Nicki smiled. "It sounds really exciting, and I'm sure it's a wonderful investment. Mario is a fantastic chef."

"Yes, he is. And I'm serious about that table. I insist, as a matter of fact."

Nicki laughed. "Well actually, Rob will be here shortly, and we happen to have dinner reservations at Mario's tonight."

Catherine clapped her hands. "That's simply wonderful! Where would you like to be seated? At one of the more intimate tables in the back? They're so romantic."

"I'm sure Rob would prefer to sit near a window, to be honest." Her boyfriend, Rob Emerson, was the assistant wine buyer for The Catalan House restaurant chain, and definitely preferred to see and be seen. Nicki couldn't imagine him ever being happy to be seated at a table in the back of anywhere.

"A window table it is." Catherine took her phone out of her purse and made a quick voice memo. Jenna would be happy to see that, considering she hadn't been able to convince either of her friends to stop using paper calendars, much less switch to electronic memos.

"So is this boyfriend the one from San Francisco, or the one who's just the wanna-be, but is a better match for you?" Suzanne pushed her shoulder-length blond hair behind one ear and smiled at Nicki. The two women were both about the same petite height with shoulder-length hair, although Suzanne's was several shades lighter than Nicki's natural, sun-streaked honey-blond.

Nicki's forehead furrowed. "I'm sorry?"

"Maxie told Frances, who told her grandson, who told his wife, who told me, that your very handsome boyfriend just might have some competition." Suzanne practically sang that last word. "From someone named Matt?"

"I'm afraid Maxie misinterpreted the situation. Matt is the editor of the magazine I write for."

"*Food & Wine Online*, I know. I have a subscription," Suzanne almost gushed with enthusiasm. "I love your articles."

"Thank you," Nicki concentrated on keeping her mouth fixed into a polite smile. She was really going to have to get Alex to teach her that trick. "Anyway, our relationship is strictly professional."

"But he flew all the way out here just to apologize, and he brought flowers." Suzanne didn't seem to be willing to let the subject go.

Making a mental note to talk to Maxie about finding something else to discuss with her friends, Nicki tried again. "It was a professional disagreement over a few articles he'd assigned to me. That's all."

Suzanne frowned. "Do all editors fly around to give apologies to their reporters?"

"Oh let it go, Suze," Catherine told her friend. "It's plain as the nose on your face that Nicki doesn't want to talk about it. Besides, her handsome boyfriend is coming into town tonight. He's the only man on her mind right now." Catherine shifted her gaze to Nicki. "We really have to go. I have another meeting in a few hours. Between managing the trusts, my exclusive circle of clients, and this new venture with Mario, I hardly have time to breathe these days."

Nicki smiled and nodded. "Of course. Please don't let me hold you up."

"Wait!" Suzanne exclaimed. "I need to get that orange-cranberry muffin recipe. For our bake sale in a few weeks. We talked about it at the last meeting. Remember?"

Nicki had a vague recollection of having nodded at a few rapid-fire requests from Suzanne. "I'll copy it for you right away."

"Can you give it to Catherine when you go by the restaurant tonight? She can drop it off at my house after she's finished her shift as the hostess at Mario's."

"Of course." Nicki added "copy the recipe" to her mental task list for the afternoon.

Catherine gave her another wink. "I won't forget about that table tonight. Who knows, it might be a big night for you." She winked again as she latched onto Suzanne's arm. "Let's go, Suze. I'll be sure to collect your recipe tonight, and we still need to say our goodbyes to Maxi. You know how long it takes you to do that."

Suzanne turned and gave Nicki one last wave before she was dragged off by Catherine. Nicki shook her head in amusement. She hoped that she never got that way with Alex and Jenna in another decade or so. As she spotted her two best friends crossing the room, heading in her direction, Nicki's smile grew. Nope. That was never going to happen.

"Sorry we couldn't get here in time to rescue you from those two. They trapped Alex and me for a good ten minutes before they moved on to you." Jenna hunched her shoulders and gave a mock shudder. "They're scary."

Alex laughed and punched Jenna lightly in the arm. "Stop. These women are Nicki's friends."

Jenna turned to Nicki and raised an eyebrow. "Is that true?"

"Most of them," Nicki hedged, then shook her head at Jenna. "Like Alex said—stop. Are you both ready to leave?"

"I'm due on shift at eleven tonight, and need to get a couple of hours of sleep before then." Alex worked in the emergency room of a hospital in the much larger city of Santa Rosa, about forty minutes west, toward the Pacific coastline.

"And I have reservations tonight at the hotel in Santa Rosa where I'll be taking my 'giant client' meeting tomorrow," Jenna said.

"My fingers are crossed for you, not that you'll need it. You're a terrific programmer and web designer, Jenna." Nicki nodded, but held out crossed fingers all the same.

"The very best," Alex echoed. "If this man doesn't hire you, then he's an idiot. Unless, of course, you slip up and call him your 'giant client' when you meet him."

Jenna's smile reached all the way across her face. "Thanks! I'm only a little nervous. I've never had a meeting with a self-made multi-millionaire before. And this contract might be huge for me."

"It's in the bag," Nicki assured her. "I'll walk out to the car with you, then come back and help Maxie clean up. She told me her housekeeper is off today."

Alex wrapped an arm around Nicki's waist as they walked toward the front door. "And you have a nice relaxing dinner with lover-boy Rob tonight."

Nicki laughed. "It would be almost impossible not to have a relaxing dinner. After all, we'll be in Soldoff, not San Francisco or New York. And on a week night. What could happen in a town with two roads, both leading into the same central square?"

CHAPTER TWO

"I DON'T KNOW HOW YOU DO IT, BABE." ROB SHOOK HIS HEAD. Not one of his perfectly groomed blond hairs budged with the movement.

"Do what?" Nicki placed her hand in Rob's as he helped her out of the car. One thing she'd always liked about Rob was his old-fashioned manners, as well as his killer smile. Which he turned on her now.

"How you can look so beautiful, classy and completely hot all at the same time." He turned the heat of his smile up a notch. "Must be some sort of witch's trick."

Nicki laughed. "Did you just call me a witch?"

Rob circled an arm around her waist and guided her toward the front door of Mario's Italian Ristorante. "Only the very best and mysterious kind, with all sorts of magical powers." He bent down and kissed her cheek. "Who knows what will happen at dinner tonight?"

Alarm bells went off in Nicki's head. *Uh Oh. I hope he won't want that table in the back after all.*

She liked Rob. And cared for him. She really did. But she was absolutely not looking for any long-term declarations from him. As they walked into Mario's, Nicki wasn't feeling nearly as comfortable as she had when Rob picked her up at her townhouse just fifteen minutes earlier. She breathed a sigh of relief when the first person she spotted was Catherine.

"Hi, Catherine. It's nice to see you again." Nicki smiled at her fellow Society member standing behind the hostess station, a stack of menus in her arms.

Catherine looked up and her lips, painted liberally in a candy-red, parted slightly as her gaze darted from Nicki to Rob and back again. "Yes. Yes. It's nice to see you again too."

"You look very chic tonight." Nicki thought the shade of blue in her blouse with the contrast of dark forest-green pants, and accented with chunky gold jewelry, suited Catherine very well.

"Thank you. Will you be wanting a table this evening?" She sent another quick glance toward Rob. "A nice quiet one in the back, perhaps?"

Nicki did a mental groan. Apparently Catherine didn't remember their conversation at the Ladies In Writing meeting just a few hours ago. Nicki opened her small handbag and pulled out a note card that had her personal stamp on the bottom. "I have the recipe Suzanne wanted you to get for her." She stepped forward and placed it on top of the hostess station, leaning in a bit as she whispered, "we decided on a table near the window when we talked at the Society meeting. Remember?"

Catherine stared at the paper for a long second before picking it up and reading it through. Finally putting it into the pocket of her jacket she glanced at Nicki. "The Society meeting. Yes. A window table." She gave Nicki a stiff smile. "I'm a little scattered tonight."

"Didn't your meeting this afternoon go well?"

"I didn't have a meeting," Catherine quickly stepped out from behind the hostess station. "I mean, my client canceled at the last minute. If you'll follow me, I'll show you to your table."

She hurried off, rapidly weaving her way toward the large front windows.

Rob leaned in close to Nicki's ear. "You asked for a seat by the window?"

Nicki smiled as she tilted her head away. "I thought a view would be nice." As soon as she said it, Nicki mentally rolled her eyes at herself. Mario's had only one floor, and the view near the window consisted of the sidewalk and parked cars. "Of the moonlight," she added. "You can't see any moonlight from the back of the restaurant."

"Well, you look great in the moonlight, babe." He placed his hand on the small of her back. "Might be more of those magical witch powers you have."

"Uh huh." Nicki sighed and sat in the chair Rob was holding out for her. She might be spending a long night dodging a conversation she simply didn't want to have. At least not at this point in their relationship.

Rob reached over and took her hand. "So tell me how you've been since we last talked?"

"You called me last night, Rob, and we talked then. Not much has happened since." Nicki smiled. If there was one thing she knew how to do, it was to get Rob going on his favorite subject. "How did your meeting go with Mr. Rossi?" Antonio Rossi was the head wine buyer for The Catalan House chain and Rob's boss. The question worked like a charm. It only took a second for Rob to be off and running on his latest plans for getting ahead in his career. Nicki listened with half an ear and idly wondered if all the males from Italy who now lived in California were named "Mario" or "Antonio". Rob's boss was Antonio and so were half of her Italian-descent classmates back in culinary school. The owner of the restaurant was Mario. A name shared by the other half of the Italian Americans in her school. Maybe she should do some research on those statistics the next time she did a piece featuring Italian wine.

"What did the detective say?"

Rob's question took Nicki off guard.

"What detective?" Soldoff was too small to have any detectives.

Its police department only had a chief, one deputy and an office clerk, all of whom she was now on a first-name basis with, thanks to finding a dead body not too long ago at a popular local winery.

"The one from New York who worked on your mother's case?"

"Oh. Detective Wilson." Nicki looked down at the linen table-cloth and bit her lower lip.

Every three months or so, Nicki would steel herself and call the NYPD detective to get an update on the progress of the investigation of her mother's murder. Which was usually to say she called just to hear the gruff, but kind, detective tell her there was nothing new to report.

Julie Connors had been stabbed to death right outside her apartment building, and her killer had never been caught. It was living with the memories that had leaped out from every corner of the city that had finally driven Nicki, along with her two best friends who loved her mother almost as much as Nicki did, to move from New York out to the West coast.

She'd made a good life for herself here, in the beautiful wine country just north of San Francisco. But what had happened to the only parent she'd ever known, right in the middle of the city she'd grown up in and had always loved, could still bring Nicki to tears just at the thought of it.

Fighting the moisture gathering in her eyes, she shook her head before looking up at Rob. "He said the usual thing. No new leads, no breaks in the case yet. He gave me a different name to call. Mom's case has been reassigned to another detective."

"Well that sounds a little encouraging," Rob's eyes and smile softened as he interlaced his fingers with hers. "A fresh perspective might be just the thing."

Nicki shrugged. "The new detective is in the cold case squad."

Rob blew out a breath and lifted her hand to his lips, placing a soft kiss on the back of it. "I'm sorry, babe. The next time I'm in New York, I can go over to the police department and talk to this new detective, if you like. See if I can get your mother's case moved to the top of the pile."

Top of the pile. Nicki sighed. That was certainly the honest way to look at it. But just thinking of it that way made her feel as if her mom didn't mean much. At least not to the New York City Police Department. Although Nicki knew better. They had tried their best, but the killer hadn't left them much to go on.

The waiter interrupted the gloomy conversation to repeat the nightly specials and take their orders. After he'd delivered a very good pinot noir to their table, Rob raised his glass to Nicki.

"I haven't had a chance to tell you that my boss was very impressed with how you solved George Lancer's murder, and he's completely forgiven you for running out the only night you managed to show up for his class." Rob grinned at her.

Tucking her thoughts about her mom away for the moment, Nicki smiled back at him while indulging in a mental shrug. "Really? How very generous of him."

———

TWO HOURS LATER AS THEY WERE GETTING READY TO LEAVE, THE restaurant owner himself stopped by the table.

"How are you this evening? I'm sorry to be so late in greeting you tonight." The short balding man with the bushy black mustache gave a slight bow from his waist. "I've had to seat the guests. Our hostess didn't return from her break, and it took my daughter until just now before she could get here to help out. The younger generation!" Mario threw up his hands in a dramatic gesture. "They're so quick to answer every message on their phones about hair-dos and boys, but not about work."

Nicki peered around the owner and glanced over at the hostess station, where am obviously grumpy Lisa was shuffling menus. "I doubt if that has changed much over the years, Mario. But what happened to Catherine?"

Mario's outstretched hands lifted even higher. "Who knows? One minute she's here instead of there, then she tells me she will be taking her dinner break at home so she's there instead of here. She needs to be more reliable."

"Well yes, of course. Did you call her?"

"I had Antonio call her. She didn't answer. She is not reliable."

"She went home for her dinner break when she works at a restaurant?" Rob snorted as he shook his head.

Nicki shot him an exasperated look before turning her attention back to Mario. "She's always struck me as being very responsible. She doesn't live far from here. Do you think you should send someone to check on her?"

"I have no one to spare." Mario sighed. "We are very busy tonight. Every chair here and in the bar is full." He gestured toward the tables behind him before giving Nicki a pleading look. "You know where she lives, yes? Maybe you could do this small favor for me?"

Rob immediately shook his head. "I have other plans for the evening."

"Which I'm sure won't suffer from making a short detour," Nicki quickly overrode Rob's objections. Other plans were certainly an acceptable excuse in the city, but not in a small town where everyone was expected to pitch in and help each other out. Aside from her career being dependent on staying on the better side of all the local residents, Nicki just plain liked them as well. "We'd be happy to, Mario. We were about to leave, so I'll have Catherine give you a call as soon as we see her."

Gathering up her purse and coat, Nicki led an annoyed Rob out of the restaurant. Once out on the sidewalk, she turned and smiled at him. "It won't take long, Rob. Her house is close enough to walk there."

Rob's frown disappeared and a gleam came into his eyes. "A walk in the moonlight sounds perfect." He took her hand firmly in his and looked around. "Which way do we go?"

Wishing she'd kept the idea of a walk to herself, Nicki pointed across the square with her free hand. "Just a block or two from here."

"Fine." Rob started off, pulling Nicki along as he headed for the dimly lit path leading through the center of the square.

"Maybe we should stick to the sidewalks," Nicki suggested. Suddenly she wasn't too keen on the idea of too much moonlight.

Rob grinned down at her. "What's a romantic walk without a little privacy?"

"It's Soldoff, Rob, not San Francisco. There's plenty of privacy on the sidewalks at this time of night." And there were also street-lights. At least that would cut down on the intimate atmosphere naturally provided by a warm dark night.

Rob swung their joined hands back and forth. "Ah, come on, babe. What objection can you have to taking a romantic walk with your boyfriend..." His voice trailed off as he stopped and stared up at the statue in the middle of the square. "Right past a giant sculpture of some grapes."

Nicki couldn't blame him for laughing. It really was a ridiculous piece of art. But she felt obligated to defend her adopted town. "Since all the businesses in Soldoff are dependent on the wine industry, the town council thought it would be very appropriate."

"What? Soldoff doesn't have any founding fathers, or war heroes, or even an artist who can create a good art deco piece?"

"The only founding father tried to sell off land he didn't own, causing a lot of headaches to the people who bought the fake deeds, not to mention the townspeople that had a parade of "new owners" suddenly showing up on their doorsteps." Nicki rolled her eyes and tugged on his hand when he laughed even harder. "Come on. Let's get to Catherine's before we're arrested for disturbing the peace."

Much to her relief, Rob started walking again. She didn't want any of the residents who might be passing along on the mostly deserted sidewalk to hear her boyfriend laughing at their statue. It was a small town, and Nicki had learned just how fast gossip could travel. Her landlady, Maxie, was the master at hearing about everything that went on in town. Nicki wouldn't be surprised if she got a call about Rob's behavior the minute she walked into her townhouse.

"Since you grew up in New York City, you have to miss the museums and night life there," Rob said.

"Sometimes." Nicki did miss all the lights and activity on occasion. But not as often as she used to. Small-town life was easy, and spending her evenings curled up in her pajamas with a good book and a cup of cinnamon coffee, had become the perfect way to end her day.

Once they'd reached the other side of the square, Nicki steered him toward one of the tiny side streets.

Rob stopped and pulled her around to stand in front of him. "Have you thought about coming back to San Francisco to live? You enjoyed the year you spent there before you moved up here, didn't you?"

Nicki sucked in a deep breath. "Yes. But I really do love my life here too. I have good friends and a growing career." She smiled. "Not to mention that fabulous gourmet kitchen Maxie put into the townhouse. I could never find anything like that in the city. At least not in my budget.

"Maybe not." Rob frowned. "But between attending all the events you write articles about and penning those novels of yours, how much time do you have to cook? Wouldn't it be nice to go out and have a gourmet meal cooked *for* you whenever you want?"

"Oh look, we're here. And see, the lights are on." Nicki pulled Rob up the short walkway and onto Catherine's front porch. After giving the doorbell a good push, she stepped back and waited. When there was no movement from inside the house, she tried ringing the doorbell again.

"The lights are on but it looks like nobody's home," Rob quipped. He took a step to the side and tried to peer through a gap in the curtains.

"Stop that. Catherine will think you're a peeping Tom." Nicki ignored Rob's offended pout and reached out to try the doorknob. It turned easily in her hand.

She opened the door as Rob stepped back to stand behind her again. He leaned down close to her ear. "I'm not supposed to look in a window, but it's okay for you to walk into a house uninvited?"

Nicki raised a finger to her lips. "Shh." She pushed the door open and took a half-step inside. "Hello? Is anyone home? Catherine, it's Nicki Connors."

She stepped further inside, with Rob following behind her.

"Now what?" he asked.

"We'll just look around to be sure she hasn't fallen or something." Nicki wandered into the living room, past a glass case filled with dolls. She paused for a moment to glance at the pictures lined up along Catherine's mantel. They were mostly shots of her and a young woman who bore a striking resemblance to Catherine, except for the bright streaks of color in her hair.

"Holy shit!"

Nicki whirled around. Rob was standing with his back to her, beneath the arched entryway into the dining room. When he didn't turn around to tell her what he was looking at, Nicki walked over to stand beside him.

Her eyes opened to a full-moon size, and she slapped her hand against her mouth to smother her yelp of shock.

There in the middle of the large formal dining table that was covered with an intricate lace tablecloth, was Catherine Dunton. She was lying with her face down in a plate of pasta, some of which was splattered across the table, leaving stains on the white lace wherever it had landed. A large carving knife was sticking out from her back.

Rob put his arm around Nicki and swayed a little. When she glanced up at him, his complexion had turned to a pasty white. As he leaned more heavily on her, Nicki quickly backed them both out of the archway and into the living room. Her petite, five- foot-two frame would be no match for Rob's almost six feet, if she counted the inch-high lifts he always wore in his shoes. If he collapsed, she'd go right down with him.

Thankfully, she managed to get him to the couch where he

sank down in a heap. Leaving him there, she fished her cell phone out of her purse and dialed the number for the Soldoff police department.

Nicki almost dropped the phone when Chief Turnlow's voice came on the line.

"Soldoff PD."

"Chief? Is that you?"

"Last time I checked it was." The chief's dry tone carried across the tiny speaker in the phone. "And this sounds a lot like Nicki Connors."

Nicki sighed in relief. At least she wasn't going to have to ask the nighttime answering service to track the chief down. "It is, and I'm at Catherine Dunton's house."

"Don't tell me she's harassing you to become a client? Do you want to make a citizen's arrest?"

Nicki bit her lip and darted a look toward the doorway to the dining room. "Um. Not exactly, Chief."

"Please do not tell me you've found another dead body, Nicki Connors." The chief's clearly annoyed tone of voice made Nicki wince.

Resigned to having to face a very irritated Chief Turnlow, Nicki sighed. "Well, now that you mention it."

CHAPTER THREE

"Tell me again why you were in this house, Nicki." The chief crossed his arms over his broad chest and gave her the stare Nicki was certain he'd perfected during his twenty years as a homicide detective on the Los Angeles police force. Topping Rob's usual six feet by a good two inches, the chief was heavy set, with a smooth-shaven face and a receding hairline. The fact was, he looked every inch a cop as far as Nicki was concerned, and she doubted if he'd ever considered being anything else. And if she hadn't gotten to know him during his last murder investigation when the two of them had bumped heads, she'd be withering away about now under that intense stare of his.

"Mario asked us to come," Rob blurted out. He'd recovered from his near-faint, and now stood with one arm around Nicki's shoulders. "He said his hostess hadn't shown up after her dinner break was over and asked us to come check on her. You can ask Mario yourself, Chief. I'm sure he'll back me up."

"I'll do that." The chief raised an eyebrow at Rob. "Mind telling me who you are?"

"I'm sorry," Nicki quickly apologized. "This is Rob Emerson. He lives in San Francisco. Rob, this is Chief Turnlow."

"I live in the Marina district." Rob held out his hand. "And I'm Nicki's boyfriend."

The chief executed a brief handshake before leaning back and looking Rob over. "Her boyfriend." He glanced over at Nicki, and now had both eyebrows raised as heat started to creep along her cheeks. "You don't say."

Rob looked between Nicki's red face and the chief's raised eyebrows and frowned. "Is there something I don't know?"

The chief shrugged. "Don't ask me. I'm the police chief, not a matchmaker."

Nicki glared at the chief while she pulled Rob to one side. "Don't pay any attention to him. It's just small-town humor. Even you've said how strange it can be. Maybe we should wait out on the porch."

Rob looked out the front window. "Wait for what?"

"What time did you two arrive?"

Nicki turned back around at the chief's question.

He had a small notebook in his hand with a stub of a pencil poised over it. "I'm assuming you came together?"

"Yes, we did," Nicki confirmed.

The chief nodded, made a note, and then pointed at Rob. "Let's start with you, Mr. Emerson." He glanced at Nicki. "Why don't you find somewhere else to be while I talk to your boyfriend. And then I'll get your statement."

Nicki instantly perked up. She'd love to have a chance to walk around. Just a little. There certainly shouldn't be any harm in that.

The chief instantly dashed her hopes to snoop a bit. "And I meant somewhere in this room. On second thought, your idea to wait out on the porch is a good one. Go ahead and do that. You can show my deputy and the coroner how to find the body once they arrive. That would be a useful, civilian sort of thing to do."

Nicki pursed her lips and huffed all the way to the front door. "What's there to show? Go in the door and turn left. It's not as if this is Buckingham Palace and you need a GPS to find your way around."

"Have something you want to add, Ms. Connors?" the chief called after her.

"Of course not, Chief. I'm going to stand on the front porch like any good private citizen would."

It was less than three minutes before Danny Findley, the lone deputy in the Soldoff police department, screeched his car to a halt in front of Catherine's neatly landscaped cottage. He waved at Nicki as he opened the trunk of the cruiser and grabbed a gym bag. Slamming the trunk lid shut, he bounded up the walkway with the ease of the top-notch linebacker he'd been a decade before in high school. His brown eyes lit up as he grinned at Nicki.

"Hi. Didn't expect to see you here." His smile suddenly drooped as he looked through the open front door where the Chief was in plain view interviewing Rob. "Isn't that your boyfriend the chief is talking to?"

Nicki sighed and nodded. She had heard more than once, and from more than one person, about Danny's crush on her. Another benefit of small-town life. Everyone knew everything about everyone else. "Yes. Chief Turnlow wanted to talk to Rob first."

"The chief said on the phone that it looked like someone had been murdered." Danny glanced around the porch. "This is Ms. Dunton's house. Is she dead? And don't tell me you found the body?"

"I'm afraid so." Nicki sighed at Danny's I-can't-believe-it tone, but had hesitated a second before answering. She had no idea if Danny had a personal connection to Catherine Dunton or not.

"She was a nice lady." Danny's tone was sympathetic but not overly upset. He took another glance into the living room. "Is your boyfriend the main suspect?"

Nicki rolled her eyes at the hopeful note in Danny's voice. "No. He isn't. He was with me, eating dinner in a restaurant filled with people who saw us both there."

"Officer Findley," the chief called out. "Get in here and bring Ms. Connors with you."

"Right away, Chief." Danny picked up the gym bag and

wrapped one hand around Nicki's upper arm. He grinned at her. "This way, Ms. Connors."

When they entered the small living room, Rob walked over and glared at the young deputy. "Hey! She's not a suspect, so there's no point in making her do some kind of perp walk."

"Perp walk?" Danny planted his feet apart and returned Rob's glare. "I'm not doing anything of the sort."

"If you two are finished, I'd like to get back to the little matter of the murder that took place here." The chief stepped forward and removed Danny's hand from Nicki's arm. At the same time, he pushed Rob back a step.

"Is everything I asked you to bring in that bag you have there?" The chief inclined his head toward the gym bag in his deputy's hand.

Danny broke his staring match with Rob to look over at the chief and nod. "Lots of crime scene tape, evidence bags and gloves."

"Good. Take that crime scene tape and start stringing it along the gate to the backyard while I talk to Miss Connors." The chief glanced over at Rob. "You go sit on the front porch. There's a nice rocking chair in the far corner. I'll send Nicki out when I'm through, and the two of you can go on home."

"Suits me fine," Rob muttered before he strode across the living room to the front hallway.

Danny slowly followed, sending Nicki a bland glance over his shoulder.

She turned to the chief and crossed her arms. "You can't blame me for the way those two behaved."

The chief shrugged. "I've seen grown men act worse over a woman. Just make sure you don't get your other boyfriend riled up so I have to take more angry phone calls from him. I don't need the headache."

"Matt is not my boyfriend, he's my editor." She crossed her arms when the chief opened his mouth. "And I don't want to talk about it. What have we got so far?"

"We? Listen, Sherlock. 'We' don't have anything. What *I* have is a crime scene that *you* happened to stumble upon. And once you've given your statement, there isn't anything else for you to do here. Your boyfriend can take you home. And I'm talking about the one sitting on the porch."

"Of course," Nicki agreed with a smile. "I just need you to excuse me for one minute."

She rushed out of the room before the chief could object. When she returned several minutes later, she found him standing over the body in the dining room.

"You ready to give your statement?" the chief asked over his shoulder.

"Yes. Then I'll go right out and wait on the porch."

The chief turned and frowned at her as he retrieved his little notebook from his shirt pocket. "You can go home, not hang out on the premises." He walked back into the living room and indicated for her to take a seat on the couch.

"Okay. Start from the last time you spoke with the victim."

Nicki went over the same story she was sure the chief had just heard from Rob about seeing Catherine in the restaurant.

The chief consulted his notes. "Why did you give her a recipe? Did she like to cook?"

"The recipe was for a muffin, so it requires more baking than cooking, but no. I've never heard her mention it. She was supposed to pass the recipe along to her friend, Suzanne Abbott. Suzanne wanted it for a charity bake sale our writing society is putting on in about a week."

Chief Turnlow nodded and turned to a previous page in his notebook. "Mr. Emerson said he didn't notice anything unusual about the victim when he saw her this evening at Mario's. How about you?"

Nicki pursed her lips. "She seemed very distracted. She didn't remember a conversation we'd had this morning, or that she was supposed to get the recipe for her friend, Suzanne." Nicki thought back over the brief conversation she'd had with Catherine at the restaurant. "Oh. She also mentioned that a client had canceled an appointment this afternoon."

"Did she seem distracted when you talked to her at your society meeting this morning?"

"No. Not at all. She was very excited about investing in Mario's."

"Oh?" The chief looked up from his notebook. "Ms. Dunton has a stake in Mario's restaurant?"

"That's what she said, Chief. It came as a surprise to me too. I hadn't heard through the gossip mill that Mario was looking for a partner."

"Is that why she'd suddenly taken up hostessing there?"

"I don't know."

"Anything else you'd like to add to your statement?" When Nicki shook her head, the chief tucked his notebook back into his pocket. "Then you can go on home. I'll be in touch if I have any more questions."

"Okay." Nicki put a bright note into her voice. "I'll just sit on the porch and wait for a ride."

The chief glanced out the front window. "What happened to your boyfriend?"

"He found this all very upsetting, and had a long drive back to San Francisco, so he left." Nicki was all innocence when the chief gave her a hard stare.

"He just left you stranded here?"

Nicki shrugged. "I told him I'd call a cab or maybe Uber."

Chief Turnlow snorted and rolled his eyes. "He's expecting you to find a cab or an Uber in Soldoff at this hour of the night?"

"He doesn't have a lot of experience with a small town. Jenna is out of town and Alex lives forty minutes away, and besides, she's working tonight. And I won't bother Maxie. She had a very long day with getting ready for the Society meeting at her house, and at her age that can sap the energy right out of you. I'm sure someone will drive by soon who I can flag down and beg a ride from."

The chief held up a beefy hand. "Enough. I'll have Danny take you home as soon as the crime scene boys and the coroner arrive." He sighed and ran a hand through his thinning hair. "In the meantime, you can walk the scene with me." He gave her another hard look. "Since that's what you were angling for anyway. You may as well make yourself useful and tell me what you see."

Nicki followed him into the dining room, trying not to smile behind his broad back. After all, that didn't seem proper under the grim circumstances.

She avoided looking at the blood spread out on the floor beneath the body, concentrating on the table instead. With only one place setting, it didn't appear Catherine had been expecting any company. There was a partially filled glass of wine next to a plate that had noodles and a creamy-looking sauce dripping over the sides from under Catherine's head. Nicki frowned and leaned in for a closer look.

"See something interesting?"

"I don't know why she'd come home to eat her dinner."

"Because she was hungry? Or maybe she preferred her own cooking to Mario's?" the chief speculated.

"But this looks like a langoustine." Nicki pointed to a curled-up lump of white meat lying next to Catherine's dinner plate.

"So she likes shrimp. Why is that unusual?" The chief frowned when Nicki shook her head.

"It's not shrimp. Langoustine is more like lobster. It mostly comes from the sea north of Ireland and is very expensive." Nicki's forehead wrinkled in thought. She looked over at the chief. "The only place that serves it anywhere in this area is Mario's."

"All right. She could have brought her dinner home to eat in peace."

Nicki nodded, but the longer she stared at the body, the more she felt that something was off. Something she couldn't quite put her finger on.

"Are you okay?"

Since the chief sounded concerned, Nicki stepped back and smoothed out her features. "Something's bothering me about this."

Her hand swept out toward the dinner table and its one occupant. "But I don't know what."

The chief moved to stand between her and the table, effectively blocking her view of the body.

"Well, when you figure it out, you let me know. Why don't we take a look in the kitchen? Maybe something in there will tell us why Mrs. Dunton chose to bring her dinner home and eat alone."

Nicki nodded but she wasn't at all convinced. Catherine had sounded too thrilled to be a part of Mario's to want to take a dinner from the restaurant home to eat, especially if the financial planner had intended on going back to her hostess job after her meal.

She walked into the kitchen and stood behind the center island, looking around as the chief came up and stood beside her. It was as neat as a pin. Not a single pot, pan or dish was out of place. Nicki glanced over at the deep farmhouse sink. Several reuseable plastic containers where neatly stacked to one side. She walked over to the refrigerator and opened the door. Except for the basic necessities, and a couple of bottles of wine which was pretty standard for any refrigerator in town, it was empty.

"Well?" The chief said from behind her.

Nicki tapped one finger against her chin before she walked over to the pantry and took a quick peek inside. There wasn't much to see in there either. Closing the door, she turned and faced the chief.

"I'm fairly certain that Catherine wasn't a cook."

The chief made a note in his little book. "Then she probably brought her dinner home with her. Which is pretty obvious since she's lying face down in it."

Nicki nodded, but something about this nagged at her. It just didn't seem right.

"Look. This has been a long and not so great night for you." The chief put an arm around Nicki's shoulders. "I gather none of your usual co-conspirators are around since you made a point of telling me that, so I want you to promise me you'll call Matt. You'll need someone to talk to."

"I'm fine," Nicki insisted, but was both mortified and surprised when her lower lip began to tremble. Biting down on it, she smiled at the chief. "Thanks for letting me look around. I'll leave the investigation to you." When he gave her a skeptical look, she laughed and held up three fingers. "Scout's honor."

"Uh huh. I'm not going to ask you if you ever were a scout. You use that door over there so you won't have to walk through the dining room and look at the body. Believe me, you'll have enough nightmares without parading past it again. Just wait on the porch while I get Danny."

CHAPTER FOUR

"THANK YOU FOR THE RIDE, DANNY." NICKI SMILED AT THE young deputy. He really was a nice guy, and she was sure once he'd gotten over his crush on her, he'd have no trouble finding a wonderful girl to plan a future with. Something she sincerely hoped would happen soon.

She remembered another visit to Mario's just a month or so ago when she'd thought that Danny and Lisa, Mario's daughter, would make a nice couple. She'd meant to mention it to Maxie, her matchmaking landlady, but in all the chaos of the winemaker's murder, she'd just plain forgotten about it. Now she decided to write it down on a sticky note the minute she was inside, so she wouldn't forget again. She hoped Maxie could fix it so Danny's puppy-dog looks would get directed elsewhere, to someone who would appreciate them.

"Are you sure you don't want me to come in and look around? Make sure everything is okay? Finding a dead body can spook a person."

Nicki opened the door to the police cruiser as she shook her head. "I'm fine. Really. And it's not the first dead body I've found."

Danny grinned. "You do seem to have a knack for it." His

mouth flattened into a serious line when Nicki let out an exasperated snort. "Chief wanted me to remind you that you should call someone and talk things out." Danny made a point of looking at his watch. "Your boyfriend's had time to get back to San Francisco by now. Guess he didn't need to call to find out how you got home."

Yep. She definitely needed to write that reminder note about Danny and Lisa.

Nicki ignored his none-too-subtle comment and stepped onto the sidewalk.

"Thanks again for the ride." She shut the car door and made short work of digging out her key and letting herself into her townhouse before Danny decided he should come in and "check around" after all. It wasn't that she didn't appreciate his concern or thoughtfulness, she simply didn't want to deal with any more questions about her boyfriend. She hadn't expected Rob to call, and probably wouldn't have been very happy if he had. She really did not want to rehash all the evening's events with him. At least not for another day or so.

Telling herself she was too tired to placate another stubborn male tonight, Nicki set her purse and keys on the hallway table and wandered back to the kitchen. It was spacious, with a big island that had room for four stools on one side, and an eat-in table just beyond it. But more important to Nicki were the beautiful quartz countertops, six-burner gas stove and whole rows of cabinets ending with a walk-in pantry on one end and a double-door refrigerator on the other. Always feeling content in her kitchen, she grabbed a wine glass off an upper open shelf and bent over to look at the selection in her wine refrigerator. After glancing over her choices, she decided to stick with the wine she'd had earlier that evening and slid out a bottle of pinot noir. The very same brand and year that she'd enjoyed at dinner with Rob. Which had ended in finding Catherine Dunton's very dead body.

Nicki sighed, finished pouring the wine, and took the glass into her office. Despite everything, she couldn't talk herself into being tired enough to go to bed. She automatically powered up her desktop computer and looked at the clock at the bottom of the screen. It was almost one in the morning. She remembered Danny's comment and felt a twinge of guilt. She should probably have called Rob and made sure *he* got home all right. He'd had a traumatic experience since, unlike her, this had been his first dead body, and then had to do a good hour's drive to get home. But it was late, and she didn't want to wake him, so she settled on being sure to call him at a more decent hour.

She pulled a pad of sticky notes toward her, grabbed a pen from the holder on the desk and scribbled out two notes — one to call Rob, and the other to talk to Maxie about Danny and Lisa. Peeling them off the pad, she pressed them to the base of her desk lamp where she'd be sure to see them in the morning, then leaned back in her chair and tapped her finger on the smoked glass surface of her desk. The chief was right. She was too much on edge from the night's unexpected events and needed to talk with someone.

But her two good friends had lives of their own, and important things going on in them. Jenna had to meet with her potentially huge client in a few hours, and Alex was busy saving lives in the emergency room of the Santa Rosa hospital she worked at. She could call Maxie, but aside from not wanting to rouse her landlady from what was probably a sound sleep after such a hectic day, Nicki also didn't want to face the lecture she'd probably get from Maxie's husband, myMason. Since Maxie always referred to the retired police chief, now master gardener, as "my Mason", running it together as if it was all one word, everyone else did too.

Nicki thought it was adorable, but since the former police chief was a man of few words, she had no idea how he felt about his new name. But she was sure she knew how he'd feel about her finding another dead body, and then calling his wife about it in the middle of the night. He hadn't been happy at all about Maxie becoming so entangled in the last murder Nicki had become involved in.

Having run through her list of friends, that only left Nicki with one possibility.

It was almost three in the morning in Kansas City where the editor-in-chief of *Food & Wine Online*, Matt Dillon, lived. She did quite a bit of freelance work for Matt's magazine, and he'd become a good friend. Of course everyone else she knew, including Chief Turnlow, thought he wanted to be more than just friends, but he'd always been professional and polite with her, so Nicki had dismissed the knowing looks and broad hints from her friends as wishful thinking on their part. And well, okay, he *had* flown out to California after she'd solved George Lancer's murder, but only because he didn't want her to go work for another magazine. It was nice to have her writing talent appreciated by her editor, just like it was to have her cooking appreciated by her friends. Besides, she had a boyfriend, and Matt certainly knew that.

She looked at the clock again. At this hour, her editor would be sound asleep and was very likely facing a busy day when he woke up in a few hours. She sighed and shut down her computer before retrieving her cell phone from her purse in the hallway. Taking it, and her glass of wine, back to the kitchen, she sent Matt a text message from her phone, then settled onto one of the high stools at the counter to finish her wine. She'd barely had a sip when her cell phone rang, causing her to jump up and dart a look around the kitchen. Putting a hand to her chest to help still her racing heart, she glared at the phone and picked it up, surprised to see Matt's name floating across her screen.

Shaking her head, she pressed the *answer* button. "What are you doing up?"

"Good morning to you too." Matt's voice was heavy with sleep. "You called?"

"I texted," Nicki corrected.

"You asked me to call you as soon as I had a free minute." He paused, and Nicki heard the distinct sound of a yawn. "I'm free now."

"You sound half asleep. I didn't mean to wake you." Nicki felt a twinge of guilt. She should have left him a voice mail on his office phone. "I hope I'm not interrupting anything besides your sleep."

"I took my date home several hours ago, and why do you get to ask those kinds of questions and I don't?" Matt sounded grumpy and Nicki couldn't blame him. She'd disturbed him in the middle of the night, and the first thing she'd done was practically ask him if he had company in his bed.

"I'm sorry. You're right. I shouldn't be asking you things like that. We can talk in the morning." Nicki was about to say "good-night" when Matt interrupted her.

"It's morning now, Nicki. What's on your mind? I thought you had a date with Rob tonight?"

Nicki frowned. She didn't remember telling Matt she had a date. "I did. But it ended a bit strangely."

"How strange?"

"We went over to a friend's house to check on her, and found her... well, we found her..." Nicki stumbled to a stop. Even she could hear the shakiness in her voice.

On the other end of the line, Matt sucked in a deep breath. "Do not tell me you found her dead."

Nicki closed her expressive hazel eyes and wrinkled her nose. "Yes."

"Nicki, listen to me. Go to your desktop. I'm going to call you on video chat. I want to see you when we talk about this." Matt waited a beat. "Can you do that?"

Even though he couldn't see her at the moment, Nicki nodded. "Sure. But we can talk about it tomorrow, Matt. Really. I'm fine."

"I'd rather have the talk now," Matt said firmly. "When I call you, promise me that you'll answer."

She smiled. He was being a bit melodramatic, which was out of character for Matt. "I'll answer. Talk to you in a minute."

Nicki heard "more like thirty seconds" before she hit the "hang up" button. Still smiling, she walked into the office and had barely taken a seat and turned on the computer when it signaled an incoming call. She clicked on the button that brought Matt's face up on the screen.

His thick mop of dark hair was standing on end in several places, with a heavy lock falling over his eyes. He impatiently swiped it away as he put on his wide-rimmed glasses with a thick black frame. Sitting there in a blue pajama top with the buttons mismatched into the wrong buttonholes, he looked like a very sleepy version of *Where's Waldo*. And those mismatched buttons told her he'd probably thrown it on just now to be decent for their call. She tilted her head slightly to one side and gave a little smile. That was too bad.

He eyed her carefully before crossing his arms over his chest. "Do you always look that good at this hour of the morning?"

"Only when I haven't been to bed yet."

"And you haven't been to bed because you found a dead body." Matt made it a statement rather than a question. "Please tell me your friend had a heart attack and died from natural causes."

Nicki sighed and shook her honey-blond hair, sending it brushing across her shoulders. "She might have. But if she did, it was caused by the large kitchen knife stuck in her back."

"You have got to be kidding me," Matt groaned. "Not again."

"I'm sorry. I told you we could talk about this in the morning after you've had more sleep." Nicki hated to admit it, but she really did feel unnerved. This hadn't been some stranger, like the last time. This time she knew the victim, and had even talked with her just hours before she was killed.

"Since I'm assuming you didn't murder her, it wasn't your fault." Matt's voice was low and soothing. "Tell me what happened, and don't leave anything out."

For the second time since she'd discovered Catherine Dunton's body, Nicki went through the entire story. When she'd finished, she was amazed at how much better she felt telling Matt. But she didn't have time to dwell on it. He immediately started asking questions the way any well-trained reporter would.

"Who did she have a meeting with that was canceled?" Matt

started out and continued on for a good five minutes. Nicki knew he was trying to get a picture of Catherine and her life in his mind. Finally he paused and smiled at her. "Okay. You next. What did you see that didn't make any sense to you?"

"What makes you think I saw anything like that?"

"Because you called me, since your so-called boyfriend didn't even bother to be sure you got home. And that frown isn't going to work, Nicki. I don't care if you told him to go, or how long a drive he had. He should have stuck around and made sure you got home okay. But the bottom line is that you didn't talk to him, and you sure can't talk to Chief Turnlow after the warning he gave you about any future interference in police business. I seem to remember that Jenna is in Santa Rosa for a big client meeting tomorrow, and Alex is probably on duty. Oh, and you would never be rude enough to wake Maxie at this hour."

"But I am rude enough to wake you?" Nicki leaned in closer as she stared at his image on the screen. It dawned on her that she had been keeping Matt very well informed about everything going on in her life.

Matt shrugged. "All part of the job. So, what's bothering you, besides finding a body of someone you actually knew, which is bad enough."

"A lot of things." Nicki sighed and flopped back in her chair. "How distracted she seemed at the restaurant when she wasn't that way at all during the Society's meeting at Maxie's house. But mostly her dinner."

"Her dinner? What was wrong with her dinner?"

"It was pasta with langoustine, so I'm sure it came from Mario's."

Matt rubbed a hand across the shadow of a beard on his cheek. "And so?"

"Why would Catherine order a dinner and take it home with her to eat on her dinner break? Why didn't she just eat it at the restaurant?" Nicki frowned.

"Maybe she needed to make a phone call or check on something at home?"

"If she wanted privacy for a call, she could have just stepped outside and walked to the end of the block. I just don't understand why she went home for a thirty-minute dinner break, where she managed to get herself killed."

"So you think she was going to meet someone?"

Nicki shook her head. "Not unless she planned on eating her dinner in front of them, which doesn't sound like something Catherine would do. The table was only set for one."

"It's possible that she surprised someone who didn't want her to know he was there."

Again, Nicki shook her head. "So she set the table, sat down, started eating her dinner, and suddenly someone who was hiding in the house decided to stab her?"

Matt furrowed his brow. "It could be that whoever was waiting for her intended to wait until she got home and just got lucky when she showed up early for her dinner break."

Nicki pursed her lips. "Maybe."

"But," Matt went on, "you don't think so." He looked up at the ceiling and closed his eyes for a moment before lowering his chin and looking back at her. "You're going to get involved in this, aren't you?"

Nicki bit her lip and looked away. "You're forgetting about the chief's warning. He specifically told me to stay out of police business."

"Somehow, Nicki Connors, I don't think that's going to stop you."

CHAPTER FIVE

THE FOLLOWING MORNING NICKI WAS SITTING AT HER DESK, contemplating whether or not to take a short break for lunch, when a familiar voice shot down the front hallway, bouncing off the walls.

"Yoo hoo? Are you home, dear?"

Smiling, Nicki shook her head and pushed her chair slightly back and swiveled around to face the open doorway. "I'm in my office, Maxie."

The click of high heels sounded on the wood floor before Nicki's landlady stepped around the portal and into the room. It was certainly no surprise to Nicki that the always perfectly groomed and dressed Maxie Edwards looked as if she'd stepped right out of a high-end beauty salon, and her flawless complexion allowed her to shave a good decade or more off her almost-seventy age whenever the need arose.

"I'm sorry to barge in on you so early, dear, but I simply couldn't wait another moment." Maxie sent Nicki a warm smile that reached all the way to her clear blue eyes.

"It's almost noon, Maxie, so it isn't that early, and I'm always glad to see you at any hour." Nicki returned the smile. Only Maxie would think anything before noon was early in the morning.

Nicki adored her landlady, who was also president of the Ladies in Writing Society. Maxie had formed the group after she'd finally abandoned her globetrotting career as a professional genealogist, to settle down with a police chief in a small town far away from the bright lights and nightlife of the big cities. But then, Nicki reflected, it's the very same thing she'd done herself, although Maxie had been pursuing love, while Nicki had been fleeing from bad memories.

When she shook her head, not one strand of her platinum-blond hair moved. "That's such a nice thing to say. But it's barely a respectable hour for a brunch and not at all the proper thing to simply drop in on someone." Her gaze shifted to the large white board that took up most of the space on one of the office walls. "I'm surprised you don't have the board half full by now."

There was no mistaking the eager note in Maxie's voice as she continued to stare at what she'd named "the murder board". The women had hung it up during the last murder they'd come across at one of the local wineries. Nicki had thought about taking it down since she wouldn't be getting involved in any more murders. But somehow, she'd never gotten around to it. And now there it was, still hanging on her wall, staring her in the face. She wasn't even a little surprised when Maxie walked over, picked up one of the markers and wrote across the top, "Catherine Dunton Murder".

"Ah. I guess you heard about the end of my dinner date last night?"

Maxie turned around, the marker still raised in one hand, and smiled at her tenant. "Of course, dear. Chief Turnlow called myMason about nine, I believe. I'm not even certain the sun was up when the phone rang."

"I'm pretty sure it was, Maxie." Nicki grinned but couldn't stop herself from getting to her feet and walking over to the board.

Her landlady's smile got bigger and she turned back to face the murder board. "Now then. What do we know?"

Nicki looked at the blank space and then back at Maxie. "We know that Chief Turnlow has sternly warned me against becoming involved in this murder investigation."

"That's ridiculous of course, dear." Maxie dismissed the chief's warning with a wave of her hand. "You found the body, so you were involved before he even arrived on the scene. And he called myMason first thing this morning. He knew myMason would tell me, and that I'd immediately drop by to consult with you. Catherine was one of our society members, so we have an obligation and a duty to find her killer. I'm sure the chief understands that, and his warning was just a formality."

"Uh huh." Nicki didn't think Chief Turnlow understood that at all, but maybe it wouldn't hurt to jot down a few things. It might go a long way to help clear her mind. Or even remember some little detail she'd forgotten to tell the chief.

Having hit upon a perfectly acceptable reason to put everything she'd seen down on the board, Nicki stepped back and planted her rear end on the edge of her desk. She studied the board while Maxie waited, her marker poised and an expectant look on her face.

"Well, we found her with her face in the middle of her dinner plate."

"What was she eating? It might be a clue." When Nicki rolled her eyes, Maxie pointed the marker at her. "In our last case, the victim was poisoned."

Giving in, Nicki smiled. "A pasta dish, with langoustine. Some of it was on the tablecloth."

"Very nice choice." Maxie lifted her marker to the board and started writing.

"She had a large knife in her back, but since she didn't have a knife block in her kitchen, I don't know if the killer brought it in with him or found it in one of the drawers." Nicki took a breath and then went on while Maxie madly printed the facts onto the board.

When Nicki had finished relating everything she could remember, she glanced over at Maxie. The older woman hadn't moved away from the board, but stood with her back to Nicki, who caught the small shudder of Maxie's shoulders. Pushing away from the desk, Nicki crossed the short distance between them and gave her landlady a hug.

Tears were sliding down the normally unflappable woman's cheeks as Nicki gently took the marker out of her hand and steered her toward the desk chair. Once Maxie was sitting down, Nicki reached into a desk drawer and pulled out a small box of tissues, holding it out as Maxie quickly grabbed several of them and dabbed her eyes.

"I'm sorry. I shouldn't have said anything about what happened. I know how much you value your friends and how hard this must be." Nicki grimaced as a bolt of guilt stabbed through her. She should have realized how hard the news of Catherine's death would hit Maxie. She'd certainly felt badly shaken once she'd arrived home and had had time to really think about it.

"Catherine was more of a close acquaintance than a friend I'd go out and have a drink with for no reason other than to catch up with each other." Maxie's voice broke as she balled a tissue up in her hand. "But underneath all that constant pushing for new clients for her financial planning business, she had a very kind heart." Maxie looked up at Nicki with a watery smile. "Although I'm sure you saw more of the pushiness than the kindness."

Nicki set the tissue box on the desk. "She pushed a little, but not so much to send me running in another direction whenever I saw her. And she always had a nice word to say about my articles and my novels. You know how much it means to writers to hear that someone has actually read what we've written."

Maxie nodded. "That sounds like Catherine. And she wouldn't have been telling a little white lie, either. If she said she'd read your novel, then she took the time to do that. She probably even left a glowing review or two. And whenever there was an event or work to be done for the Society, her hand was always the first one raised. And I could count on her to follow through on whatever task she took on."

With a heavy sigh, Maxie glanced over at the board. "With her divorce final and renting that cute little house right off the square, she was finally getting a handhold on some happiness. And then someone literally put a knife into her back." The older woman looked up at Nicki, her eyes still wet but lit with determination.

Nicki had a feeling what was coming next.

"We owe it to her to find out what happened and bring the culprit to justice!" Maxie rose to her feet and wrapped her well-manicured fingers around Nicki's upper arm. "We didn't stand by when that detestable winemaker was murdered, and we certainly won't when the victim is one of our own."

Feeling both trapped and slightly elated, Nicki nodded. She couldn't possibly say "no" to Maxie. After everything her generous landlady had done for her, there simply wasn't any choice. But right now, it would be best if Maxie took a break from the murder board.

Since Nicki had had so much trouble sleeping the night before, her day had started a good six hours ago and only with a cup of coffee. Realizing she was famished, Nicki knew it was an excellent excuse to get Maxie out of her office and into the kitchen where there were no murder boards to stare at.

"Why don't we take a break and prepare some lunch?" Nicki turned her head and glanced out the window toward the front lawn and side-by-side driveways. Her on-its-last-legs, robin-egg-blue Toyota sat on one side, and normally Jenna's equally worn out Honda sat on the other since she rented the townhouse next to Nicki's. Maxie had given them both a phenomenal deal to live on her large property in the section everyone in the area called her "writer's colony".

The little enclave with six townhouses, in sets of two, scattered around a wide circular road had been a huge boon to Nicki, and to her very tight budget, as she got her freelance writing and budding novelist careers off the ground. Nicki's budget was tight enough it didn't lend itself to taking on a new car, and the monthly payment that went with it, since she still had bills to pay from her move from New York to California, and for her mother's funeral expenses. Not to mention the student loans she'd taken out to attend college and then culinary school.

Julie Connors' estate hadn't extended beyond a small bank account and her personal possessions in her apartment, none of which would have covered the cost of a funeral. Nicki would have asked her father for help, but she had no idea where he was, or how to get hold of him. He'd completely disappeared from her life when she was five years old.

"It's a bit early for lunch, but a brunch would be perfect," Maxie said, bringing Nicki's attention back to the present. "Does your pantry extend to mimosas? I would like a drink, and I've been wanting one of your mimosas ever since yesterday when we suffered through Suzanne's concoction."

Nicki bit the inside of her lip to keep from smiling. Poor Suzanne wanted to be a gourmet cook so badly, but had blinders on when it came to ingredients. If a recipe called for tomatoes, Suzanne saw no difference between using fresh ones or something that came out of a can. She had the same approach to herbs and spices.

"You're in luck. I just picked up some fresh oranges that are in the refrigerator cooling nicely, and I'm sure I have a Cava in the wine fridge." Nicki would enjoy a glass of sparkling wine from Spain.

Maxie straightened her spine and nodded. "Perfect. Let's whip up a delicious bite or two and have a toast to Catherine."

"That sounds just right." She linked her arm through Maxie's and winked at her landlady. "If there's something in particular that you'd like to make, I'll do my best to scrounge up the ingredients for it."

That got a small laugh out of Maxie, who then gave Nicki's

hand a gentle pat. "Oh no, dear. I'd never presume to cook in your lovely kitchen."

"Since you're the one who paid to have it renovated, I'm sure that gives you the right to cook in it." Nicki smiled and waited for Maxie's next protest. She knew that Maxie had a full-time cook and housekeeper. As far as Nicki had observed the few times she'd seen Maxie in her own kitchen, her landlady was a bit vague on how to turn on the stove, much less how to use one.

"That was so you could put to use that degree from culinary school that you have, and I would be able to be one of your fortunate guests to taste your meals."

Nicki laughed as the two of them stepped into her very high-end kitchen. "You're welcome to dine here any time. And so is your husband."

"Why that's very nice of you, dear. As soon as you tell me you'll be making meatloaf and potatoes for dinner, I'll be sure to let myMason know," Maxie chuckled. "And do not go ruining it by putting anything green on the plate. It would be such a tremendous letdown for the poor man."

"Meat, potatoes, nothing green. I'm sure I can manage that." Nicki rounded the large center island and headed for the refrigerator. "Since we'll be having mimosas, how does an egg and mushroom omelet sound? I have some wonderful fontina cheese to go with that." Nicki started taking things out of the refrigerator and setting them on the nearest counter. She opened one of the drawers and handed oranges to Maxie who was standing behind her, peering over her shoulder.

"Here. You can cut up the oranges if you don't mind. I'll get the Cava in a minute."

"That's quite a bit of food you've gathered, dear." Maxie took the oranges over to the island and reached for a knife from the butcher block on the counter.

"I'm going to make a little extra in case Jenna shows up soon. If she doesn't, I'll keep it in the fridge and reheat it for dinner. I'm sure she'll be back by then."

The two women worked quietly together, exchanging an occasional smile. Nicki listened to several of Maxie's anecdotes about Catherine, determined to save her questions and any murder discussions until after their impromptu brunch. She carefully placed the egg dish on plates as Maxie poured the fizzy orange drink into two champagne flutes. They had barely sat down on tall stools pulled up to the center island when the front door banged shut, sending its echo reverberating all the way back to the kitchen.

"Hello? I'm back. You'd better be here, Nicki Connors, because I have some great news."

There was another loud thud, which Nicki assumed was Jenna's overnight bag hitting the floor. Next came the sound of flip flops rapidly smacking their way down the hall.

"We're in here, Jenna," Nicki called out which wasn't necessary at all since her good friend appeared in the doorway barely a second later.

At the huge smile on the self-proclaimed computer nerd's face, Nicki set her glass down and clapped her hands together. "You got the contract!"

"I did," Jenna crowed. "It couldn't have gone better, and you are now looking at the web designer for Trident Industries, with facilities in four states and a gazillion dollars in annual sales." She took a small bow when Maxie and Nicki broke into applause.

"So everything went along without any bumps, dear?" Maxie patted the seat of the stool next to her.

Jenna sank down and leaned back, her untamed mass of black frizz and curls cascading over the back of the stool. "Not a single bump made an appearance. It was the absolute ult experience, and I never want to go through that again. I was so nervous, I swear I could hear my knees knocking together." She looked at the plates on the counter and grinned. "And I'm just in time for lunch. Please tell me you made some extra."

"I did." Nicki slid off her stool to prepare another plate.

Jenna grinned and mouthed an exaggerated "thank you", before turning her attention to Maxie. Her brown eyes behind the oversized frame of her glasses narrowed as she studied the older woman's face. "What's wrong?"

Maxie sighed and looked over at Nicki. "I really do hate to ruin such a wonderful moment."

"You didn't ruin it, Maxie," Nicki snorted. "Whoever killed Catherine did."

Jenna's hands instantly shot up. "Whoa. What? Someone killed Catherine? Catherine who?"

"Catherine Dunton, dear. I believe you met her at the Society meeting."

"Of course I know her. She's been trying to make me one of her clients." Jenna frowned. "Someone murdered her? When?"

"Last night." Nicki walked over and put a plate with a mushroom omelet and creamy cheese melted down its side in front of Jenna.

"Last night?" Jenna glanced over at the big clock hanging on the far wall beyond the upper cabinets. "Word gets around quick." She turned back to Maxie. "Did Chief Turnlow call your husband about it?"

Maxie nodded. "Yes, he called this morning. But I wish Nicki had told me last night. I would have insisted she come spend the night at our house, instead of staying here alone."

Jenna slowly turned toward her friend, a fierce frown on her face. "And how did you happen to find out about it last night?"

"Oh, Nicki found out about it before the chief did." Maxie ignored the slight groan from Nicki.

Jenna crossed her arms on the counter and dropped her head on top of them. Her muffled voice was still clear enough for Nicki to hear. "Do not tell me you found another dead body."

"It wasn't just me," Nicki was quick to put in. "Rob and I both found her."

"Oh, I'm sure lover-boy was a real big help," Jenna lifted her head and reached into her back pocket. Shed pulled out a cell phone.

"Who are you calling?" Nicki asked.

"Who do you think?" Jenna responded then leaned away as Nicki made a grab for her phone. "Hey, glad I could catch you. Do you remember meeting Catherine Dunton at the Ladies in Writing meeting yesterday?"

Nicki closed her eyes when Jenna paused for a moment, listening to the person on the other end of the line. "Uh huh. The financial planner. Well, it seems she was murdered last night."

Jenna cut a glance over to Nicki and rolled her eyes, ignoring the frantic waves from her friend. "And Alex, you'll never guess who found the body."

CHAPTER SIX

"LUNCH WAS EXCELLENT, NICKI." MAXIE CAREFULLY DABBED A napkin against her mouth.

The three women were gathered in Nicki's office, and Maxie had settled herself into the chair Jenna had carried in from the dining room that was between the main living area and the kitchen.

Nicki plopped down into her desk chair and handed Jenna the marker. "Since you couldn't wait to tell Alex all about our latest case, you can do the honors of standing at the board and writing down our 'to-do' list."

Jenna grinned at her and grabbed the marker, waving it over her head. "That's fine. Your handwriting is almost as bad as Alex's. And she didn't seem all that surprised at the news."

Nicki crossed her arms and narrowed her hazel eyes. "I could hear her scream right through the phone, Jenna."

"You're exaggerating. It's a writer thing. And if you think she was loud on the phone, wait until she hears you calling this 'our latest case'."

"I'm afraid she's right, dear," Maxie put in before Nicki managed to get another word out. "Alex *was* rather loud. Even I could hear her say she would be here this evening as soon as she got off her shift."

"She's only racing over here because she has three days off and wanted an excuse not to have to do any wedding shopping with her mom." Jenna shrugged as she turned toward the white board. "Alex will do just about anything to get out of any kind of wedding shopping. I think she's still pushing for a destination wedding with only their immediate families invited." Jenna turned her head to smile at Nicki. "Which includes us, of course."

Nicki nodded. "Of course." The three of them had been a family ever since they'd shared a tiny apartment in New York while they'd pursued their separate careers. After Nicki's mom had been murdered, Jenna made the decision for both herself and Nicki that they would get away from New York and follow Alex out to her home state of California, where she was doing her residency after medical school.

Alex had been thrilled to have her friends back with her, and the move across the country had proved to be exactly what they'd all needed. Nicki loved New York City, but had finally come to accept that she could no longer live there. Too many memories, no matter what subway she took or street she walked down. After three years, she'd come to call California her home.

And one of her best friends falling in love had been the icing on the cake. Especially when she really liked the man who'd asked Alex to marry him.

Alex had now been engaged to Tyler Johnson, a solidly built, amiable fireman who worked for the City of Santa Rosa, for almost six months. And while Alex had made it very clear that she wanted a small, easily organized wedding on a beach somewhere, she'd been ganged up on and out-voted by her fiancé and her mother. The two of them had an entirely different vision that included a church, a reception, lots of flowers, and of course a wedding dress. Which Alex had yet to buy despite the fact her wedding was rapidly approaching the six-months-from-now mark.

Nicki thought the good doctor might not get around to it until the week before the big day, no matter how hard Alex's exasperated mother pushed her to go dress shopping. Luckily Tyler was like most men and didn't really care what his bride would be wearing, as long as she showed up for the event itself and the honeymoon.

Thinking Jenna was probably right, and Alex was coming for a three-day visit to get out of being dragged to every bridal shop in town by her mother, Nicki glanced over at Maxie.

"You knew Catherine best. Did she mention anyone she'd had an argument with lately, or maybe a dissatisfied client?"

Maxie pursed her lips as her eyes scrunched at the corners. "I didn't know her well enough to have that kind of cozy chat with her." She sighed and shook her head. "I didn't take the time to do that when I should have."

Jenna turned around and looked at her landlady. "Don't beat yourself up about that. It's impossible to be on a 'cozy chat' basis with everyone you meet."

"I second that, Maxie." Nicki reached over to give her a comforting pat on the shoulder. "Catherine had a lot of friends here, and I'm sure she'd be happy that we're going to do everything we can to find out who killed her."

Maxie nodded and sat up straighter in her chair. "Of course, dear. And it's the least we can do for her, so we'd better get started."

Satisfied that Maxie seemed to be holding up okay, Nicki turned back to Jenna. "I think our first 'to-do' should be to talk with Suzanne Abbott. She might be able to tell us quite a bit about anything unusual going on in Catherine's life lately."

Maxie immediately perked up even more. "That's an excellent idea. Catherine and Suzanne were practically inseparable. They were closer than Catherine was to her own twin."

Nicki and Jenna exchanged a raised-eyebrow look before focusing back on Maxie.

"Twin? I didn't realize Catherine had a twin," Nicki said. "At least I don't recall Catherine ever mentioning it."

"Oh, they weren't close, and if you saw them standing side-by side you'd never know they were twins. Cynthia is very different from Catherine." Maxie gave a decisive nod. "I rarely see Cynthia myself. She's a retired librarian, but has never shown an interest in writing anything herself. She lives in Sonoma."

"Sonoma," Jenna repeated as she madly scribbled across the white surface of the board.

"That's only twenty minutes from Soldoff." Nicki thought that would be an easy enough round trip for a murder.

Sonoma was the bigger, much better-known wine city in the county. With its large plaza surrounded by small businesses that fed on the year-round tourist trade, it had been the model used by Soldoff's town council to design its own central square. Although Sonoma's boasted a statue of General Vallejo who'd helped found the town, which would probably seem more appropriate to a casual visitor than a ten-foot high bunch of grapes sculpted in bronze.

"Yes, but I doubt if the two visited each other much," Maxie said. "But Suzanne would know about that."

"How about other relatives?" Jenna tapped the marker against the board. "I think she mentioned a recent divorce when I talked to her at the meeting yesterday."

"That's right. And I believe her ex-husband still lives in town." She glanced over at Maxie. "And doesn't she have a daughter in college?"

"Walter Gifford." Maxie pointed at Jenna. "You should add his name to the list. Aren't ex-husbands always the first to be suspected in these circumstances?"

Nicki's eyebrows winged up in surprise. "Walter Gifford? The same Gifford who has an art gallery in town? He's Catherine's ex-husband?"

"Yes, he is," Maxie confirmed. "He also has a gallery in San Francisco and in Los Angeles, and a few other cities as I recall. He's done very well for himself."

"I'm definitely putting the ex-husband on our list." Jenna

printed out "Walter Gifford" right under the name of Catherine's twin sister. "And you said she had a daughter in college?"

"She mentioned her to me once. I believe her name is Ramona." Nicki's brow furrowed in thought. "That was a while ago, so she may gave graduated by now."

"I doubt that, dear." Maxie shook her head as her blue eyes took on a small sparkle. "She's been in school at least six or seven years. Catherine did confide to me that Ramona seemed to be making a career out of being a student."

"She should also go on the list until we confirm whether or not she's still away at school," Nicki told Jenna, who dutifully added Ramona's name to the board.

The tall, dark-haired web designer stepped back and gazed at the board. "It's not a long list, but Suzanne might be able to add a few names." She glanced over at Nicki and Maxie. "Unless you have others to add? Business associates maybe?"

Nicki sighed and curled in her bottom lip. She hated the thought, but she was sure Chief Turnlow would add the friendly restaurant owner to his interview list. "Mario, unfortunately. Catherine had just become an investment partner in his restaurant. She was working there as the hostess the night she died."

"Oh." Jenna frowned. "So anyone who was there that night would have known when she left."

Maxie lifted a hand to her throat. Nicki knew that the older woman had a soft spot for the very outgoing, and very talkative, Mario.

"I'm sorry Maxie." Nicki sent her a sympathetic look. "But I'm sure the chief will also be questioning him, and any of the staff who were there last night."

"Of course he will, dear. But I'm sure Mario is perfectly innocent in all of this." Her lips, which still retained the exact shade of red that matched her earrings and her shoes, curled upward at the corners. "I remember saying much the same thing about several of the winery owners in our last investigation, and I was right about them. I'm sure I'm right about Mario as well."

"I doubt if he's involved, but we still need to talk to him. He might have heard Catherine mention that she was meeting someone."

Maxie smiled. "Now wouldn't that be nice?"

"And very convenient." Jenna snapped the cap back onto the top of the marker. "I'm guessing we should start tomorrow by talking with Suzanne. And by 'we', I mean you and Alex. I have to work on a preliminary plan for my new client's website tomorrow."

Nicki blew out a breath as she thought about the three chapters she needed to finish in her latest Tyrone Blackstone, Superspy, novel, not to mention several articles she'd promised to have done as part of her freelance writing work. She also needed to complete a new entry for her personal blog, *Nicki Knows*, about the food and wine scene in Northern California.

Maxie made a sympathetic humming sound in her throat. "I know you girls are very busy with your computer things and writing, but it's important that we see this to the end. I don't want to let Catherine down."

Nicki flashed Jenna a questioning look, gratified when her friend nodded.

"The wonderful part about computer things and writing is that we can do them any time of the day or night." She swiveled around and tapped on the screen of her desktop computer which immediately came to life. "I'll work on rearranging my schedule and then let Matt know if I need some extra time for the *Food & Wine Online* articles. He said he'd be fine with it."

Nicki closed her eyes when Jenna pounced on that statement.

"He did?" She carefully set the marker down and grinned at her friend. "You've already talked to Matt about this new case of yours? When did that conversation take place?"

"Hopefully last night, dear." Maxie lifted her shoulders up and back in a graceful stretch. "Since Bob left her at Catherine's to make her own way home, she'd need someone to talk to after such a traumatic evening."

Jenna crossed her arms and sent Nicki a narrow-eyed stare. "Lover-boy left you stranded?"

"Rob. His name is Rob," Nicki corrected patiently. When did everyone around her take to mispronouncing things? "And I told him to go home."

"Not that I don't agree with the sentiment, but why didn't you have him drop you off first?"

"Because I knew the chief would be sure I got home, and I was hoping he'd let me see the crime scene while we were waiting for the coroner."

"Which he did," Maxie confirmed with a nod to Jenna. "And he suggested she call Matt. Which I'm now happy to hear that Nicki did."

"Must have been pretty late in Kansas City." Jenna grinned. "Did your wanna-be boyfriend answer the phone on the first ring?"

"No, he didn't," Nicki sniffed. "As a matter of fact, I woke him up, so we didn't talk long at all." Nicki felt like she should cross her fingers. They hadn't talked long, at least not if you considered an hour as a short conversation. "And he doesn't want to be my boyfriend," she added out of habit.

"Of course he does," both Maxie and Jenna sang out in perfect unison, causing Nicki to roll her eyes heavenward. The two of them, along with Alex, were like a broken record when it came to her relationship with her editor.

"No he doesn't," Nicki stated firmly. "And we need to get back to business. I think Alex and I should talk with Suzanne first." She smiled at Maxie. "Would you like to come along?"

"Oh no, dear. I'm sure Suzanne would be much more open around the two of you without me along. But I will set up an appointment for us to talk with Walter."

"All right. And I'll get started on some double fudge brownies" Jenna laughed. "For Suzanne, I take it?"

"Nothing helps get you through a sad time like chocolate," Nicki declared.

"Uh huh." Jenna winked at Maxie. "Nicki could get a stone statue to talk by offering it one of her double fudge brownies."

"It's an excellent idea," Maxie agreed. "And with Alex coming tonight, that should complete the conversation."

Nicki frowned. "I'm not sure if Alex had a chance to meet Suzanne at the meeting yesterday."

"Oh no, dear. I'm not talking about Alex having a conversation with Suzanne. I meant your wonderful doctor friend's conversation with you." Maxie stood up and smoothed out the lightweight jacket she was wearing. "There's no one better than Alex to get to the bottom of that early hours' conversation you had with Matt."

Jenna laughed while Nicki slapped a hand to her forehead and groaned out loud.

Pulling her phone out of her back pocket, Jenna sent her friend a wicked smile. "I'll just text her now to let her know she needs to ask you about it."

CHAPTER SEVEN

Nicki and Alex chugged along in Nicki's old blue Toyota. Alex was concentrating on her cell phone as she tapped the address of Suzanne Abbot's house into the GPS app on her device.

"There. I think I've got it." Alex nodded in satisfaction as the tinny-sounding, programmed voice began to give out directions. Placing her cell on top of the cracked vinyl of the dashboard, she glanced over at Nicki and smiled.

"As much as I can't believe you tripped over another dead body, I can't tell you how glad I am *not* to be out dress shopping today." She pushed back a lock of her dark brown hair that had fallen across her forehead. "Although if mom calls you, be sure to tell her that we have your dire emergency under control, and she shouldn't worry."

"Dire emergency?" Nicki made a tsking sound. "Are you saying you lied to your mother?"

"Not lied. I'd say a dead body is definitely an emergency."

Nicki shot her friend a skeptical look. "So you want me to tell your mother that I found a dead body?"

Alex gave a hard shake of her head. "Absolutely not. Tell her a friend passed away, and you needed help to make the arrangements."

"What arrangements?"

"Well. We did arrange to meet with Suzanne this morning, didn't we? That counts."

"That's really stretching it Dr. Kolman, soon-to-be Doctor Johnson, unless of course there's no ceremony because you never bought a dress." Nicki negotiated the turn from Maxie's property onto the highway, as the GPS chirped out directions from its precarious position on the dashboard.

"Stretching, maybe, but not a lie. And it turns out one of the local boutiques has a website, so I'll do my shopping online and simply order a dress in my size, and that will take care of that. Mom can come along for the fitting so she can have her mother-of-the bride experience."

Nicki bit her lower lip and kept her eyes glued to the road in front of her. Every once in a while she was reminded of all the things she would miss out on, like arguing with her mom over wedding dress shopping. But she wasn't going to have that chance, and her mom would never be the mother-of-the-bride.

"I'm sorry, Nicki. I know you'd give anything to be able to go wedding dress shopping with your mom." Alex reached over and squeezed one of Nicki's hands that was tightly gripping the steering wheel. "I miss her too."

Nicki managed a shaky smile for her friend. "I know you do. And so does Jenna. And I don't want you to hold back telling me anything about your wedding because you're worried it will make me sad. I'm so happy for you and Tyler that I want to hear everything." Her smile grew steadier. "Promise me you won't hold back?"

Alex held up her right hand. "I solemnly swear to tell one of my best friends in all the world, who is also going to be one of my maids-of-honor, to bore her to tears over every little detail of this wedding."

Nicki laughed. "Well you can leave out a few. I don't want to hear about any celebration moments between you and that hunky fiancé of yours."

"From what Jenna texted, we might be exchanging a few celebration stories, or was she kidding when she wrote that you spent an hour on the phone with that adorable editor of yours in the wee hours of the morning." Alex leaned back and arched one eyebrow at her friend. "I'm supposed to get every detail out of you."

"There aren't any more details." And there really weren't. She'd already told Jenna about the call, and she knew Jenna had relayed the information to Alex. "I called him when I got home after finding Catherine. We talked about it and he gave me the expected lecture on not becoming involved in police matters. I didn't make him any promises on that."

"Hmm. So you don't find it unusual that he answered the call?"

"Why wouldn't he answer the call? He's my editor."

"Maybe because it was three o'clock in the morning and you didn't call and leave a message on his office phone. Or are you going to tell me he was at work?"

"No," Nicki groused. "He wasn't at work."

"Was he alone?"

"That, Alex Kolman, was none of my business, It would have been beyond rude for me to ask him something like that." Nicki lifted her chin and put a tinge of outrage in her voice. Unfortunately her friend knew her too well.

"Well, did you ask him?"

Nicki deflated a bit and sighed heavily. "Maybe. But not directly and not on purpose. And it's still not any of your business."

"Maybe. But any man who is so interested in you to be alone on a Saturday night and take your phone call at three in the morning is definitely my business. And Jenna's and Ty's, too. And Maxie certainly feels she has some say-so in your life as well."

"And," Alex continued before Nicki could open her mouth. "We have a say-so because we all love you. It's the same reason why you grilled Tyler the first time you met him."

Unable to deny that little fact, Nicki gave an exasperated snort just as the voice from the GPS warned her to make the final turn onto the street where Suzanne lived. A minute later she stopped the car in front of a neatly landscaped house in the old Spanish-style architecture favored throughout the wine country.

"This is her house." Nicki twisted around and reached into the back seat for the plate filled with double fudge brownies before she stepped out of the car and joined Alex on the walkway.

A large archway led to the double-sided front door. Nicki pressed the doorbell, then waited as she heard heels clicking across the floor on the other side.

When Suzanne opened the door, the first thing Nicki noticed were the tears in her eyes. Judging by the puffiness in her face, Nicki guessed the poor woman had been crying from the minute she'd been told about Catherine's untimely death.

"Come in," Suzanne sniffled, holding a tissue to her nose.

Nicki stepped inside and gave Suzanne a half smile. "Thank you for seeing us. I'm so sorry about Catherine."

"Thank you. I made coffee."

Alex and Nicki followed Suzanne down a long hallway and into a large living space with a fireplace at one end and the kitchen at the other. Suzanne stopped at the dining table where there was a tray with cups and a large silver pot sitting on its highly polished surface.

When Suzanne stood and stared at the pot for several long moments, Nicki put an arm around her shoulders and urged her to sit down.

"Why don't you let me take care of the coffee? We can have it with the double fudge brownies I brought." Nicki set the covered plate on the table and telegraphed a look to Alex. Not needing any words to understand, Alex immediately reached for a cup and the coffeepot.

"Here, let me pour this out. You've both had a very difficult couple of days." Alex set a cup in front of Suzanne and arranged the creamer and sugar bowl next to her while Nicki unwrapped the plastic from the plate holding the brownies.

"Chocolate doesn't cure anything, but sometimes you just need a bit of it," Nicki said gently.

Something between a laugh and a sob escaped from Suzanne. "Catherine would have so approved of that. She was always trying to get me to indulge in desserts, and I was always giving her lectures about healthy eating. I'm going to take up running in the mornings very soon. Catherine was trying to talk me out of it. She thought I was crazy. She said I'd probably drop dead from a heart attack and then what would she do without her best friend?" Suzanne paused and dragged in a ragged breath. "She never told me what I was supposed to do without mine."

Nicki's eyes went moist. Suzanne was clearly grieving deeply about Catherine's death, and she just could not bring herself to ask her questions and possibly overwhelm Suzanne with memories.

"We wanted to stop by and let you know we were thinking about you as well as Catherine." Nicki smiled. "I liked her very much, and just wanted to say that."

"She liked you." Suzanne looked up and nodded at Nicki. "She always said you were smart and kind and pretty. She called it the perfect combination. Is what you said at the Society meeting true? Did you really figure out who killed that winemaker?"

"Yes she did," Alex put in quickly.

"I helped Chief Turnlow solve it," Nicki corrected. "And I'm sure he'll do everything he can to find out who killed Catherine. He was a homicide detective in Los Angeles for twenty years, so he knows what he's doing."

"That's right, he does," Alex added her assurances as well when Suzanne turned her head to look at both of them.

"But you're going to help him, aren't you? I mean, you helped with that winemaker and you said you didn't even know him. But you knew Catherine. And you liked her. You just said so." Suzanne's hand grabbed onto Nicki's wrist. "Someone in her family did this. Or someone she knew, and you have to find out who it was."

Nicki leaned away and blinked several times before raising an eyebrow at Alex.

"It could have been a passing stranger," Alex pointed out, then did her own raised eyebrow when Suzanne violently shook her head.

"Someone ungrateful killed her, I'm sure of it. No one in her family appreciated what she did for them. The same can be said for a few people outside of her family." Suzanne grabbed a brownie and took a good-size bite, chewing and talking at the same time. "Well, except for Charlie. He never said a mean thing to her. If he had, she would have told me right away."

"Charlie?" Nicki prompted.

"Her boyfriend. For the last few months she'd spent a lot of her spare time at his winery."

"Charlie Freeman?" Nicki found herself blinking again when Suzanne nodded as she popped the last of the brownie into her mouth and, without missing a beat, reached for another one.

The lovable older man who owned Charlie's WineTime Winery was Catherine's boyfriend? Charlie was one of the truly beloved locals who'd made Soldoff his home for several decades, and had been making the worst wine in the state, and probably the country, for almost as long. He also brought it to every wine event he was invited to, and since he was such a long-time resident, Charlie was invited to them all. He always offered a glass to everyone, and if you were his friend, or wanted to be accepted as a member of the community, you drank every drop.

Nicki had tried a number of his blends, and had even visited his winery. Fortunately the setting for the tasting room was beautiful enough, and the small bites offered to go along with the wine were tasty enough, that she had given it an honest mention in one of her articles for *Food & Wine Online*. At least for the ambiance and the food. She'd diplomatically not mentioned the wine at all.

"He isn't at all like Walter I'm-so-much-better-than-all-of-you

Gifford. Now *he's* a real piece of work." Suzanne stabbed at the air with her forefinger, as if she was poking the man in the chest, or an eye. She practically glared at Nicki. "Isn't the ex-husband usually the culprit? That could certainly be true here."

"Divorces can get very nasty," Alex quietly agreed. "But it doesn't lead to one spouse killing another as often as you'd think."

"It might when you mix it with money." Suzanne finished the second brownie and picked up a third, studying it for a moment before taking a bite. "Catherine was his wife *and* his financial planner. When one of the funds she put his money into took a bad turn, he lost at least one hundred thousand dollars before she managed to get him out of it. He was so angry he went out and had an affair with some bimbo half his age, and then asked Catherine for a divorce when she found out about it and went ballistic. He said *she* wasn't being reasonable. Who has an affair and then claims his wife is the unreasonable one?"

Suzanne's eyes were lit with fire and her mouth twisted downward. She left no doubt that she had less than zero love for her best friend's former husband.

"So the ex-husband is definitely on the list," Alex commented in a dry tone, earning her a warning glance from Nicki.

"You said she had other family?" Nicki prompted when Suzanne had settled into fuming silently.

"Ramona. Her ungrateful daughter she had with her first husband, Stewart Newton. She's a twenty-six-year old brat who seems to think she's entitled to live off on her own with the bucks from home, as long as she enrolls in a class or two and claims to be a student. Seven years she's been at college, and she came home last month and told Catherine she was going to change her major. Again. Threw a tantrum like a two-year-old when Catherine told her she wouldn't pay for it anymore." Suzanne reached for another brownie. "My own daughter is getting ready to leave soon for college. I've already warned her about pulling that same stunt on me."

Suzanne's eyes narrowed as she chewed. "And Catherine should have told Cynthia the same thing she told Ramona when her sister asked for extra money from their father's trust to buy another of those first-edition books she likes so much."

"Cynthia is Catherine's twin, isn't she?" When Suzanne's eyes opened wider, Nicki smiled. "Maxie told me that Catherine had a twin. I was surprised, since I'd never heard Catherine mention a twin before."

"She rarely mentioned Cynthia to anyone. They didn't look alike, and certainly didn't act alike. About the only time they communicated was over the phone once a month when they went over the balance of the trust their father left to them. He'd named Catherine as the executor, but she made sure Cynthia got a regular report along with a monthly allowance. Other than that, they weren't close. But then she didn't see or talk to her daughter much either. Unless Ramona wanted money."

Suzanne shook her head, so her heavily highlighted, honey-blond hair swung back and forth over her shoulders. "The people who should have cared about her the most, didn't really care about Catherine at all."

CHAPTER EIGHT

AN HOUR LATER NICKI SLID GRATEFULLY INTO HER LITTLE Toyota. She pressed the door-lock button so Alex could climb into the other side. Nicki leaned back and silently gripped the steering wheel. She'd had no idea that visiting Suzanne would be so exhausting. The woman had constantly bounced between tears, smiles and rage. Once Alex had settled into her seat, she also tipped her head back against the headrest.

"That was certainly intense. And a little on the weird side." Alex's eyes were closed and her arms hung limp at her side.

"It definitely had a high level of stress." Nicki rolled her shoulders before turning the key, doing her usual automatic prayer that the engine would start. When it coughed, sputtered for a moment or two, and then died, she sighed and tapped her fingers against the steering wheel.

"If it won't start, we're walking from here. I am *not* going back into that house to ask for a ride into town." Alex crossed her arms and shook her head.

"That's fine talk from someone who took a full rotation in psychiatry." Having waited the mechanic-recommended thirty seconds, Nicki turned the key and tried again. This time the engine started right up and purred as if it had just come off a new-car lot. If cars could have persnickety personalities, hers definitely had one. "She's understandably upset and having a really bad reaction to losing her best friend."

"That behavior was more obsessed than upset. And trust me, I know, since I *did* take that rotation on the psychiatric floor during my second year of residency." Alex turned to look at Nicki. "Did you notice the way she was dressed?"

"Not really. Why?" Nicki backed out of the driveway and gave an inward sigh of relief as they headed up the road. She hadn't wanted to go back in and ask Suzanne for help either.

"I swear you have almost that same outfit in your closet. The colors were slightly different, but it was a fairly good match. I wouldn't have noticed except she wore a replica of that blue dress you own to the Society meeting brunch the other day. I thought it was just a coincidence, but now I'm not so sure."

"It was just a dress, Alex. Lots of women own clothing in that shade of blue."

Alex twisted around even more in her seat so she was directly facing her friend. "And the same type of jewelry and shoes? She almost has your hair color, and I'd bet she'd have the exact color if she could duplicate your sun-streaked look from a bottle, and she definitely has your haircut. And didn't you say that she's trying to become a gourmet cook, just like you? What does she write to qualify as a member of that society? A food and wine blog, by any chance?"

"She's writing a spy series that she hopes to get published." Nicki knew that was only going to fuel Alex's "obsessed" theory about Suzanne.

Her friend rolled her eyes. "Don't tell me. She named her main character T-Bone Brownstone, a secret cousin to your superspy, Tyrone Blackstone."

Nicki laughed. "Now you're going way too far out there. I have no idea what she's named any of her characters, and her main character might be a female for all I know. But I'm sure she didn't name him or her 'T-Bone'."

"Seriously, Nicki. Sometimes you have a hard time seeing what's right in front of you unless it concerns a dead body. Like Matt's keen personal interest in you that goes way beyond being your editor, and Suzanne's bizarre mimicking of how you dress and what you do."

"I think you've all beaten the subject of Matt to death. He's never even suggested a coffee date, much less some kind of keen interest. And he only flew out here to give me flowers because I'd threatened to start writing articles for his competition after he'd acted like such a jerk. So we don't need to go over all that again. And as far as Suzanne is concerned, she's probably just searching for an identity since her daughter is getting ready to go off to college."

"Searching for an identity because of an empty nest?" Alex laughed. "Have you been reading those FBI profiling books as part of your research for those spy novels?"

Nicki grinned. "Maybe."

"I'm just saying that if you're making a list of suspects, put her on it." Alex's phone chirped, and she quickly picked it up from her side pocket. Nicki knew by the ringtone that it was Jenna calling.

"Hello? Yes, she's right here." Alex glanced over at Nicki then smiled. "Probably on her kitchen counter, but you can ask her yourself." She pressed the speaker button then held the phone closer to Nicki so they could both hear what Jenna had to say.

"Where's your phone, Connors?" Jenna's voice filled the small interior of the Toyota.

A picture suddenly flashed into Nicki's mind of plugging her cell phone in to charge it, and promptly walking off and leaving it behind when they'd left the townhouse.

"Probably on the kitchen counter like Alex said. Why?"

"Because Chief Turnlow called me. Apparently it's more acceptable to interrupt a mere web designer than a doctor." Jenna's tone was definitely leaning toward the frustrated side.

Nicki and Alex exchanged a grin.

"Having trouble with your draft plan for that giant client?" Nicki could sympathize since she'd struggled over hundreds of proposals for books and articles.

"Only because of the interruptions."

"How many interruptions have you had?" Alex asked.

"Just one, and stuff it, Dr. Smarty-Pants."

Nicki stifled a laugh. She could picture Jenna crossing her arms and glaring at the phone from behind her large glasses. "Okay. I gather your one interruption was from the chief. What did he want?"

"He was trying to track you down. He said he wanted to see you in his office right away."

Puzzled, Nicki's eyes narrowed in thought. She couldn't imagine what the chief wanted to talk about that was so important that she had to make an immediate appearance in his office.

"If he arrests you for murder, let me know. I'll bring bail money. After I finish this preliminary design plan."

Nicki snorted as Jenna hung up. "Gee, thanks."

"Of course I'll also be happy to contribute to your bail fund," Alex said with a perfectly straight face.

"And gee thanks to you too," Nicki retorted. "I don't know why the first person on the scene is always a suspect."

"Because they *were* the first person there and usually leave their fingerprints all over the place. But aside from that, is there any other reason the chief would want to see you?"

"I haven't the foggiest idea." Nicki turned her little car onto the street that went around the town square. The small building housing the Soldoff police department sat on a corner at the opposite end.

"But I guess we'll find out soon enough."

They fell into a companionable silence as Nicki maneuvered around the square and pulled into one of the two public parking spots in front of the station. Fran, the long-time department clerk, waved a greeting to them when they walked in the door.

Nicki was pretty sure Fran had been at the police department almost as long as Soldoff had decided to fund one of its own, rather than rely on the county sheriff. And it wasn't because crime was a real problem with the residents, so much as keeping the peace during the many food, art and wine festivals held in the town each year. On those weekends, hundreds, and sometimes thousands, of visitors poured into town to enjoy the festivities, and to take advantage of the dozen or more wine tasting rooms located around the square.

"Hello, girls. How are you doing this beautiful day?" Fran rose on her toes to look over the front counter at Nicki's empty hands. "I don't see any treat bag, so I guess you aren't here to bribe me for any information."

Nicki blushed as she returned Fran's smile. She guessed she hadn't been as subtle with her previous orange muffin offering as she'd thought she'd been. "Hi, Fran. You remember my friend, Alex Kolman?"

"Sure do. I recall I told her to go over and apply for a job at Sandy's diner. Of course, I didn't know she was a doctor then." Fran grinned showing the gap in her teeth on the right side which, along with her frizzy gray hair, only added to her image as a comforting grandma, a role Nicki was sure Fran had been called upon to play on more than one occasion.

"I should have brought a bribe," Nicki said as Alex shook Fran's hand. She leaned over the counter and asked in a loud whisper, "do you have any idea why the chief wanted me to meet him at his office?"

"I do." Fran nodded and winked at Nicki. "But I'm going to keep myself out of hot water this time and let him tell you."

"Thank you, Fran." Chief Turnlow appeared in back of his clerk. He stood with his hands clasped behind his back and a trace of a smile on his lips. "I appreciate that." His smile grew when he glanced over at Alex, "Hello, doctor."

She inclined her head in his direction. "Chief."

"You can join us if you'd like to. I have a feeling you'll be interested in what I have to say to Ms. Connors." He gestured toward his office before turning and disappearing back inside.

"Uh oh," Nicki whispered to Alex. "This can't be good if I'm back to being 'Ms. Connors'."

"Did you forget to pay a parking ticket?" Alex whispered back.

Nicki gave her an exasperated look before giving a toss of her head that sent her honey-blond hair bouncing over her shoulders. Determined not to be intimidated by the chief, she marched around the front counter and down the very short hallway.

The chief's office was so small there was barely room for a desk, a file cabinet and two visitor chairs. Since he was already seated behind his desk, Nicki and Alex took the visitor chairs. Nicki crossed her arms and stared at the Soldoff Chief of Police.

"So what did I do to make this an official visit?"

The chief's thick eyebrows drew together. "Why do you think this is an official visit?"

"Because you called me Ms. Connors rather than Nicki?"

"If I said Nicki Ann Connors, would that make the reason for this visit clearer?"

"Not unless my mother was saying it." Nicki frowned. "What's this about, Chief?"

Chief Turnlow leaned back in his chair, which creaked and groaned before going silent. He folded his hands across his chest and shook his head at her. "Let's see if I can do a reasonable imitation of a parent. How many times have I asked you to get that boyfriend of yours under control?"

"This is about Rob?" Nicki was completely astonished. Why in the world was the chief annoyed with him? Nicki knew Rob well enough to guess he'd most likely found a reason to get on a plane for a scrounged-together business trip, so he could get as far away as he could from any connection with a murder. That kind of talk wouldn't be good at all for his career.

The chief let out a huge, clearly exaggerated sigh. "Not that boyfriend. The other one."

"He means Matt," Alex supplied in a loud stage whisper. "The one who has no interest in you."

"I know who he means." Nicki narrowed her gaze on Alex before turning back to the chief. "He's my editor. Not my boyfriend. He doesn't have a personal interest in me. And you were the one who suggested I call him after I found Catherine's body."

"I only meant that you needed someone to talk to."

"Which is what I did. I can't help it if he called you after he talked with me."

The chief shook his head. "He didn't call me. He came to see me."

"What?" Nicki jumped to her feet. Matt dropped in on the chief? She couldn't have heard that right. But there the chief sat, nodding his head.

"That's right. That editor, who doesn't have any personal interest in you, strolled right in here about an hour ago and wanted to know if I had any new information about the Dunton murder. By your reaction, I'm guessing he didn't let you know he was coming, but I can't believe he didn't call and tell you he was here. Because if he had, I assume you would have discouraged him from dropping in on the local police."

"She left her phone on the kitchen counter," Alex supplied before dissolving into laughter.

Nicki poked her friend in the arm with her index finger. "Stop that. This is ridiculous. He's supposed to be getting ready to go to the food and wine festival in Los Angeles. It's the biggest one on the West Coast. How's he going to be there, when he's here?"

"I've heard there are planes that fly between San Francisco and Los Angeles on a fairly regular basis." The chief chuckled at the glare Nicki aimed at him. "Maybe Matt thought he'd stop by and grill the local police chief on the latest murder case before he flew off to his food festival."

Nicki plopped back into the visitor's chair and began to tap her fingers against the arm. She thought it was more likely that Matt had come to be sure she was staying out of trouble. Then what the chief had said sunk in.

"He grilled you on the murder? What did you tell him?"

The chief straightened up and leaned his elbows on top of his desk. "If I tell you, will you promise to get him to stay out of my office and my investigation?"

Nicki rolled her eyes but nodded her agreement. She would tell Matt. She certainly couldn't promise that he would listen though. That stubborn streak he'd developed during the last murder she'd become involved in, seemed to have taken up a permanent residence with her editor.

"Okay." Chief Turnlow smiled at her. "I told him I haven't found out anything yet. I don't have the coroner's report, and the evidence is still at the forensics lab. I talked with her daughter. She came to the house and verified that it didn't appear anything was missing, which includes the cash and credit cards that were still in her purse. I'm going to pay a visit to Mario and his staff as soon as we've finished our little talk, since the restaurant is the last place Ms. Dunton was seen alive. And that's everything."

Nicki slowly nodded, thinking it through. "If nothing was stolen, then Catherine must have been murdered for a personal reason."

"Or you and boyfriend number one scared the murderer off, and you were lucky not to have been killed yourselves," the chief pointed out. "And I'd appreciate it if you wouldn't spread any rumors. I'd hate to see the folks in this town start to look at each other funny."

"After you talk to Mario, are you going to go see Walter Gifford, her ex-husband?" Nicki asked.

"That's right, and that's enough talk about this murder." The chief huffed out a breath as he pushed himself to his feet. "Now you keep your end of the bargain and go talk to Matt. He's probably left you a half-dozen messages by now. I'm surprised he hasn't called your friends to try to track you down."

The words were barely out of the chief's mouth when Alex's phone rang.

CHAPTER NINE

"WHAT ARE YOU DOING HERE INSTEAD OF SCHMOOZING WITH the famous artists and chefs at the L.A. Food and Wine Festival?" Nicki had spotted Matt in the bar that took up the whole bottom floor of the Sorenson, a three-star, ten-room boutique hotel tucked into an arbor-lined area just off the square. She hadn't even taken a seat before she'd tossed the question at him.

"I came to see how my best freelance writer is doing." Matt smiled up at her before rising and pulling out a chair. He stepped back with a flourish of his hand and a slight bow at the waist.

Exasperated but reluctantly charmed by his silly gesture and boyish grin, Nicki lowered herself into the chair and leaned back as she crossed her legs under the small, round table. Matt signaled to the lone bartender who nodded. A few moments later he brought over a glass of one of Nicki's favorite chardonnays. She took a sip before she began to drum her fingernails against the tabletop.

"Have you developed some kind of telepathy that told the bartender to pour a glass of one of my favorite wines?"

Matt's grin stayed in place as he shook his head, sending a thick lock of dark hair tumbling down his forehead. "Nope. Chief Turnlow called and said you were on your way here."

"Oh?" Nicki's eyebrow went up a notch. "What else did the chief say?"

Matt took a long slow sip of his beer. "That I should brace myself. You didn't seem too happy when you left his office."

"I wasn't," Nicki confirmed, determined to lay down a few ground rules for her editor. He couldn't pop in and out like a piece of bread in a toaster anytime the mood struck him. And especially whenever he thought she might be doing something he didn't want her to do. He and Rob couldn't have been more opposite when it came to that. Brushing away the unexpected comparison with her actual boyfriend, Nicki studied the man sitting across from her.

"So why are you here instead of in Los Angeles?"

"I can get to Los Angeles from here easily enough. I'm sure there's a plane or two going that way." The hand holding Matt's beer stein paused in midair when Nicki scowled at him.

"So I've heard. What I haven't heard is why you're here at all."

"You really are pissed about that, aren't you?" Matt's mouth turned down at the corners as he carefully set the beer stein down. "Am I to take that as a message that you just don't like seeing me?"

Now Nicki's gaze progressed to a full-on glare. "Don't be such a dense male, Matt. Of course I like seeing you. I just don't like you checking up on me because you think I'm getting into trouble behind your back."

Nicki did a silent count to ten when Matt's grin settled back into place.

"Oh, I don't need to be here to check on whether or not you're getting into some kind of trouble. When it comes to finding a murder, I *know* you are. I came to help out in a pinch."

"Help out in a pinch? What pinch?"

Matt shrugged. "The one where Jenna is busy trying to impress her newest, and very big client, and Alex has to stay in Santa Rosa to save all those lives, not to mention to keep her fiancé happy. And I'm sure Mason is going to keep a closer eye on Maxie this time around, now that he's on to what the four of you were up to over George Lancer's murder."

"We weren't 'up' to anything except talking to a few people."

"And got a threat to your life. Or have you forgotten that part?"

Judging by Matt's sudden frown, it was clear to Nicki that *he* hadn't forgotten about it.

"So what kind of help are you proposing?" she asked cautiously.

"To be your sidekick. I know my schedule for the event in Los Angeles. I have one of the assistant editors covering most of it. And for the three times I need to make a personal appearance, I've got them all lined up for the same day, so it will only need to be a down-and-back. I'll be gone one day and two nights at the most."

"It's nice you feel you can trust me on my own for one whole day." Nicki rolled her eyes but it was only for show. The truth was, he'd brought up good points about her friends and their current schedules, so she wouldn't mind his help at all. It would also save her a lot of late night or early morning phone calls, since she would have talked to him about it anyway. Then another thought struck her.

"Jane isn't coming, is she?" Jane was Matt's very efficient, and very scary, admin assistant. Nicki did her best to avoid any video or phone contact with her, and only communicated by e-mail.

Matt laughed. "No. Jane isn't coming. She's going to hold down the fort in Kansas City while I try playing Dr. Watson to your Sherlock Holmes for the first time."

"First time? Don't you mean the only time?" Nicki pushed away from the table and stood. "Alex is having coffee over at Starbucks. I need to pick her up before going home, so I'll meet you at the townhouse."

"I wish I believed it would be the last time you'd get mixed up in a murder," Matt muttered, then hastily made a lot of noise as he got to his feet when Nicki looked his way.

"Did you say something?" Nicki's polite expression didn't give a hint that she'd heard every word. Honestly. How many dead bodies did Matt think would be showing up in Soldoff in the future? Nicki had thought her first one would also be her last, but she was positive *this* one would be. It was Soldoff, for goodness sakes. Not New York.

———

"DID YOU AND MATT WORK THINGS OUT?" ALEX ASKED ONCE they were on their way to Nicki's townhouse.

"More or less. Actually, I have no idea if we worked anything out, but we did come to an understanding."

"Which was?"

"He's going to help out with the investigation on the days in between having to make an appearance at the L.A. Food and Wine festival. Which turns out to be only one day. And his admin is going to stay in Kansas City." Nicki shrugged. "With you and Jenna so busy with your own schedules, it will be nice to have someone to help distract Maxie."

Nicki sighed. "My landlady feels responsible for solving Catherine's murder, since she was a member of her Ladies in Writing Society. And I suspect I won't get a moment's peace from Suzanne until Catherine's killer is locked up."

"So Matt thinks he's going to be playing the macho bodyguard, when you're secretly going to have him run interference with Maxie and Suzanne?"

Nicki grinned. "He can be pretty cute. Women fall all over him whenever we've been at festivals together."

"Since men fall all over you, there must have been bodies everywhere at those festivals," Alex teased.

Nicki had always acknowledged the beautiful face she'd inherited from her mother, along with a perfect figure on a petite frame, but she had never been impressed with her own looks. So she rarely noticed if anyone was falling all over her, and if her face and figure were the only reasons, she ignored those men anyway. Just like she ignored Alex's observation about her appeal to the opposite sex, and focused on her 'bodyguard' comment.

"Matt called himself a sidekick, not a bodyguard. I think that's a better description of his role."

"Did he happen to mention which day he'll need to be in Los Angeles?"

"No. But the festival starts this coming Wednesday and goes through Sunday, so I'm assuming he'd need to be there Friday or Saturday." Nicki gave Alex a suspicious look. "Why?"

"I'm betting it's Saturday, because I got a call from Ty while I was having coffee. It seems my hunky fireman has next weekend off all of a sudden, and since I do too, he thought we should come here and spend the night and hang out with my best friends. He wanted me to check with you to be sure it was okay."

Nicki could not believe it. Matt had arranged for another big strong male to be around for the one day he was going to the festival?

Alex dug her phone out of the side pocket of her purse and started tapping keys.

"Who are you texting?" Nicki fervently wished she hadn't left her phone sitting on the kitchen counter.

"Tyler Johnson. I'm asking if he's talked to Matt recently, as in the last two days."

"Good." Nicki stepped on the gas. "I guess Mr. Dillon and I have something else we need to discuss."

It took them another ten minutes to reach the turnoff to Maxie's property, and another two minutes before they pulled up in front of Nicki's townhouse. Matt was outside, leaning against the door of the SUV he'd rented, talking to Maxie and Jenna. Nicki got out of her very compact car and concentrated on not slamming the door. She deliberately strolled up to Matt and smiled when he looked at her.

"Mathew Dillon. Have you talked to Ty lately?"

Matt crossed his arms over his chest and stared right back at her. "Uh huh. And he's coming to stay here while I'm in L.A." Matt glanced over at Alex. "He didn't mind since we both know Alex will make some excuse to be here too, if the rest of you are running off to investigate a murder. Isn't that true?"

Alex crossed her own arms. "Maybe."

"Oh give it up, you two." Jenna shoved her unruly mass of hair back over her shoulder. "Matt already confessed that all your manly men worked it out after the winery murder that if we ever got involved in another one, they were going to make sure at least one of them was with us at all times." She threw her hands up. "We can't stop them, so we may as well put them to work."

"It would have been nice to have been asked first," Nicki said pointedly to Matt, who didn't bother to hide his grin.

"No point in that. You'd have said 'no way', and we would have come along anyway, so it was faster to just go ahead and coordinate all our schedules and skip over the arguing."

Giving up, for the moment at least, Nicki motioned toward the townhouse. "Let's go in and I'll make a big pot of coffee. We need to update the murder board with all the information we got out of Suzanne and the chief."

"The chief? He told me he didn't have anything," Matt complained as the group trooped into the house and down the hallway toward the kitchen.

They gathered around the large island while Nicki took out several bottles of water and the coffee grinder from one of the cabinets. "He said Catherine's daughter didn't find anything missing."

"Ramona's in town?" Maxie frowned. "I thought she was spending her summer with friends in Europe. At least that's what Catherine told me."

"Apparently not. The chief said she went by Catherine's house to check if anything was missing, and nothing was. Even her cash and credit cards were still in her purse, which I noticed was in plain view on the kitchen counter."

"So a robber wasn't after something quick and easy." Matt ran a hand over the side of his face.

"Or it wasn't a robbery at all," Jenna put in. "What are you thinking, Nicki?"

She looked up while the coffee beans were grinding away and smiled. "I'm thinking we should add all the suspects Suzanne gave us to the murder board, and then maybe get ready to go out and have a bite to eat."

"Go out?" Alex blinked. "Wouldn't it be better to order in salads while we talked all this out?"

"You get your salad, I'm getting a burger."

Jenna had a huge weakness for a good hamburger, and the greasier the better. It was a constant source of good-natured argument between her and the health-conscious Alex, with Nicki usually siding with one or the other, depending on her mood.

"A hamburger sounds good," Maxie said. "But I'm thinking Nicki has a sudden craving for Italian food?" She beamed when Nicki sent her a wink and a nod. "I'll call Mario's and put in a reservation for..." Maxie hesitated as she quickly did a count of bodies in the room. "Five, since myMason is playing poker with his friends tonight."

"The earlier the better, Maxie," Nicki said. "Alex has to drive home tonight because she's on duty tomorrow."

"Thanks," Alex said. "I also want to be sure you put Suzanne on the suspect list."

"What?" Jenna and Maxie asked in unison as Alex vigorously nodded her head.

Nicki handed several mugs to Matt. "The coffee's ready," she called out to get their attention. "Matt can pour, and then we'll all go into my office and talk a little bit of murder."

CHAPTER TEN

"WHAT WOULD ANYONE RECOMMEND?" MATT ASKED THE GROUP as he opened the menu at Mario's Ristorante, which was located very inconveniently, for anyone but wine-tasting visitors, in downtown Soldoff. But despite that daunting drawback, it still drew enough clientele from the bigger cities of Sonoma and Santa Rosa to do a brisk business, even on a weekday night.

The decor inside was both rustic and cliché, with wine decanters surrounded by plastic grapes adorning the walls in between paintings of scenes in Rome, Venice and a number of other picturesque cities in Italy. One wall had a large portrait of Mario, his wife and two children, standing in front of the famous Trevi fountain when it was lit up at night. Lisa, Mario's oldest daughter, had shown them to their seats, batting her eyes at Matt the whole way much to his embarrassment and the obvious enjoyment of his four female companions, who'd trailed behind with wide grins on their faces. Lisa had managed to even linger at the table for several minutes until their waiter had shooed her back to the hostess station near the front door.

"Everything here is pretty good," Jenna said in response to Matt's question. "And since three of us here, anyway, are used to the really superior Italian restaurants in New York City, that's saying something."

"Unless you've eaten at Osteria Francescana." Nicki smiled. "It might be the best Italian restaurant in the world."

Alex's eyes sparkled just a little as she looked at Nicki. "Really? Are you planning on dining there any time soon?"

"Not at those prices." Nicki inclined her head at her landlady. "Maxie's eaten there."

"You have?" Jenna raised an eyebrow at the older woman. "How much did that set you back?"

Maxie laughed. "Oh, I'm sure the meal was well over five hundred dollars for two, and probably closer to one thousand with the wine. But I didn't pay for it, of course. One of my genealogy clients did. She's Swiss, extremely wealthy, and was very pleased with my work."

Jenna shook her head in disbelief while Maxie turned a sunny smile on Matt.

"Our editor friend here has also eaten at Osteria Francescana. And probably more often than I have."

Matt hunched his shoulders and hid behind his menu.

Nicki blinked and then stared at him, her hazel eyes wide with surprise. "You have?"

Jenna reached around Nicki and pulled down the top of Matt's menu. "Hello? Want to tell the rest of us peasants how you managed to dine out at a thousand-dollar restaurant not once but several times?"

"My grandmother lives in Italy," Matt mumbled.

Nicki continued to stare at him. "You have an Italian grand-mother named Dillon?"

Heaving a big sigh, Matt adjusted his glasses and looked around at the four faces turned in his direction. "No. I have an Italian grandmother named Gaspari. It was my mother's maiden name."

"And Lucia is as charming as her grandson." Maxie nodded as she picked up her menu. "But a great deal richer, of course."

Matt's face turned a fire-engine red, and he slumped down in his chair even more as he shot Maxie a glare. Nicki smothered her laughter as Matt looked every bit like a ten-year-old boy who hated being the center of attention for all the wrong reasons.

"Oh sit up and be the gentleman I know you are, dear," Maxie admonished. "If you're going to pursue Nicki, then you'll have to tell her something more personal sooner or later. You can't always discuss the business of running an online magazine, and you certainly can't expect to talk only about food and wine forever. That won't get you anywhere."

"Well. That's certainly putting it right out there." Jenna lifted her wine glass in a salute to Maxie while Alex coughed discreetly into her napkin.

Nicki didn't think it was possible, but Matt's face turned even redder. He looked positively miserable, and she felt more than a little twinge of sympathy. She shook her head at Maxie who was perusing the menu, apparently oblivious to the very uncomfortable Matt sitting next to her.

"Maxie, stop teasing him. He's outnumbered and, as you said, way too much of a gentleman to contradict you in front of other people." Nicki shifted her gaze from her landlady to Matt. "Don't pay any attention to them. We tease each other all the time. If you want to stick around and be Dr. Watson, then you'll have to get used to it." She quickly picked up her menu and dropped her voice to a loud whisper. "Shh, everyone. Here comes Mario. Remember why we're here."

"To get something to eat?" Jenna was still grinning at Matt when Alex gave her a nudge under the table with her foot.

"Shh," Nicki repeated before putting on a properly sober look as Mario came up to the table. Short and slightly balding with a large belly, Mario had a snow-white apron tied around his waist. He showed a toothy smile underneath his drooping mustache.

"Nicki, Nicki!" He grabbed one of her hands and clasped it to his chest with both of his. "I should have called you to be sure you were all right. I shall forever feel like a goat for sending you to check on poor Catherine rather than go myself." He gave her hand a hard enough squeeze that it almost brought tears to her eyes. "Can you ever forgive me?"

Matt suddenly stood up and stuck out his hand. "I'm Matt Dillon."

Nicki gave a sigh of relief when Mario was forced to let her hand go in order to shake Matt's.

"Since I have already met the boyfriend on several occasions here at my ristorante, you are her brother?" Mario looked from Matt to Nicki. "Or a cousin perhaps?"

"Not hardly," Jenna murmured right before Nicki cut her off.

"He's my editor at *Food & Wine Online,*" she quickly supplied along with a sharp warning glance at Jenna. She wasn't at all surprised when Mario gave Matt's hand another enthusiastic shake. After all, Matt Dillon's online magazine had a large subscriber base, and a word of praise on its website was worth a lot of business to that fortunate restaurant or winery.

"You are *that* Matt Dillon," Mario gushed.

Nicki lifted a hand to hide her smile. Matt's mother had been a big fan of the old TV western, *Gunsmoke,* and named her son after the leading character, Marshal Matt Dillon. Nicki doubted very much if Mario had ever heard of anyone else by that name, so she was fairly certain her editor was the only "Matt Dillon" that Mario had ever met.

"I should have known when you came in with Nicki. Are you here on business?"

"Not tonight," Matt told an immediately crestfallen Mario. "But I'll be in town for a while."

"Mario." Maxie drew his attention away from the magazine editor. "Won't you sit down for a few minutes and keep Nicki company while Jenna and I give our visitors a short, lovely tour of the square? I promised Matt I would show him our world-famous grape statue." Maxie rose and pulled Alex up with her.

"Great idea." Jenna got to her feet and jerked her head at Matt. "Let's go see what the grapes look like at sunset."

"Yes," Alex chimed in, turning a megawatt smile on the restaurant owner. "Nicki's still distraught from finding Catherine the way that she did. And barely six months after the last body she stumbled across. It would do her a world of good to be able to talk to you."

Matt put his hands on the stuttering Mario's shoulders and all but shoved him into a chair next to Nicki. "Thanks. We appreciate it, and I'm sure Nicki will too."

Nicki rolled her eyes when she heard Maxie say, "Don't you think that was a little harder than necessary, dear?" And even kept her smile in place at Matt's curt "no" before he ushered all three women out the door. She looked out the big window that was behind Mario, and watched them cross the street that was still busy with late afternoon traffic before disappearing into the square.

"I'm sorry you had such an upset." Mario gave her hand lying on the table a firm pat. "It must have been very unpleasant."

"It was. And shocking." Nicki lowered her voice and quickly put her hand in her lap to keep him from giving it another bone-crunching squeeze. "Mario, I don't understand why she went home? When we found her, it looked like she was eating her dinner. But why didn't she eat here?"

He gave an expressive shrug of his shoulders. "It was her dinner break. Maybe she didn't want to spend her dinner break with the rest of us. I didn't ask her."

"Did she always order food from the restaurant and then take it home to eat during her dinner break?"

Mario's eyes squinted a bit. "She didn't take any food home with her. At least not from my ristorante."

"Are you sure?" Nicki pressed.

He gave another shrug. "I walked to the door with her to find a time when we could talk some business. She only had her purse. No food."

Nicki frowned. She wouldn't have left it in her car because her house was an easy walk from the restaurant. And Nicki was sure that pasta was from Mario's. "Is there another restaurant in the area that serves langoustine?"

"Certainly not." Mario puffed his chest out and raised his chin. "No other restaurant from here to San Francisco serves it besides Mario's. Have you seen such a fine meal somewhere else?"

"No, I haven't." Nicki filed that away as she tried another topic. "Catherine told me she'd bought an interest in your restaurant." She ignored the sudden stiffness in Mario's expression. "She also said you wanted to buy it back." Which was a little stretch of the truth. Nicki had actually learned that from Suzanne during the distraught woman's litany of ungrateful acts against her best friend.

"This is my son's legacy. I never should have allowed an outsider to buy a piece of it." Mario looked away and Nicki spied his clenched fists which weren't quite hidden by the tablecloth. "I explained this to Catherine, so she would understand and sell her interest back to me."

"Did she agree?"

"Not yet, but I'm sure she would have very soon." Mario returned his gaze to Nicki's face. "That last night, she asked about my son. She wanted to know if he was going to take extra classes in the wine section of his culinary school." A smile slowly crept onto his lips. "He is going to the Institute of Culinary Education in New York. One of the best schools in the world. It's where you went, yes?"

"I did." And she had, going from earning her Creative Writing degree at Columbia, straight into a top culinary school right there in the city. Nicki had never regretted a minute of the time she'd spent there, or the cost of the student loans she was still paying off. "So Catherine didn't usually ask about your family?"

Mario shook his head. "She liked to talk business, and sometimes about her writing. I'm certain she asked about my son because she understood when I explained this restaurant was his legacy, and eventually she would sell back her part of it."

"Why did you sell her an interest in Mario's in the first place?"

"The school in New York is very expensive, and one of our ovens broke at the same time that we had a leak in our roof. Both had to be fixed just when the school tuition must also be paid. What could I do?" Mario spread his hands wide and his mustache seemed to droop even more than usual. "Even though those things were fixed, I knew I'd made a terrible mistake, so I offered to make payments, with interest, until she was paid back every cent of her money."

"But she turned you down?"

Mario shrugged. "She would have changed her mind. I could tell when she asked about my son."

Once again Nicki deliberately switched to another subject. "Did she seem a little off that evening? When Rob and I came in, she appeared to be a bit flustered."

"I thought the same thing when she didn't seat the Hobsons at their usual table. I had to move them and apologize, and of course offer them a complimentary glass of wine. When I asked Catherine about it, she said she was distracted because she was expecting someone at her house later that evening." He gave Nicki a wink. "I think she meant Charlie was coming over to have a drink, and possibly breakfast the next morning, yes?"

Nicki frowned. "Did she say she was expecting Charlie?"

"No. But she was so nervous it could only be in anticipation of a wonderful evening." Mario lifted his hands and suggestively wiggled his eyebrows.

Nicki fought to keep from rolling her eyes. Somehow a visit from Charlie just didn't evoke the same blissful images for her that Mario was clearly imagining. The long-time winemaker was too much of an old-fashioned gentleman for her to see him as some kind of elderly Don Juan.

Seeing Mario glance around the room, Nicki doubted she'd be able to keep his attention any longer, so she thanked the owner for his time and asked if he'd send their waiter over. As soon as he left the table, her friends walked back through the front door, making Nicki suspect they'd been watching the whole conversation through the front window.

"Well. Did you get what you needed?" Matt asked once they were all settled and their dinner orders had been taken.

Nicki nodded. "Catherine didn't have any food with her when she left the restaurant, so she must have already had it at home and simply heated it up."

"Which means she left Mario's to go home and eat leftovers from Mario's?" Jenna shook her head. "Too weird."

"I agree, dear," Maxie said. "Catherine was no cook, as far as I knew, and she'd said on more than one occasion that there was no point in eating at home if you could eat out. I think she would have qualified even heating up a meal as eating at home."

They were interrupted by their waiter bringing their soup and salads. Once he'd set each plate and bowl in front of the proper person, he looked at Nicki with a bare wisp of a smile.

"I don't mean to bring up a sad subject to ruin your meal, but I overheard you talking with Mario about Catherine. I only want to say how sorry I am she was killed. And even sorrier that a nice lady like you had to find her like that."

"Thank you, Joe." Nicki gave an audible sigh. "I wish I knew why she'd gone home on her dinner break. It just seemed like a strange thing to do."

Joe hugged the large tray he'd carried the food on close to his chest. "Well. She'd been acting strange since she arrived. She called Mario and said she'd decided to come in earlier than planned and hostess that night, so he sent Lisa home. But she only stayed an hour or so before she went on her dinner break. And was more trouble than help during that hour, so we all mentioned we were glad she'd taken a break. Now everyone feels really bad about that."

Maxie made a clucking noise with her tongue. "There's no way you could have known what would happen, Joe. It wasn't anyone's fault, and you shouldn't feel that way."

"No, it wasn't." Nicki's voice was quiet and full of understanding. She knew from personal experience how guilty someone could feel if they thought they could have prevented another person's death. Hadn't she carried that same guilt around with her for almost a year after her mother had died? Shutting the thought out, Nicki concentrated on the present. "You mentioned Catherine had been acting strangely? In what way?"

"She seated too many people at one server's station and not enough at another. And like Mario told you, she forgot where some of the regulars like to sit." Joe looked down for a moment before bringing his gaze up again and offering a smile to everyone at the table. "I should check on your order. If you need anything in the meantime, just give me a signal." He sent another sad-looking smile to Nicki before turning around and heading back toward the door leading into the kitchen.

"So she was acting wonky around everyone," Jenna observed once Joe was out of hearing range.

"Did you find out anything else from Mario?" Matt kept his voice low and leaned in closer to Nicki.

She propped her elbows on the table and rested her chin on one hand. "He was trying to buy back Catherine's interest in the restaurant, but he didn't have the money, so he offered to make payments with interest."

"That sounds like a reasonable offer." Alex nodded as she took a very small bite off one end of a breadstick. "Did she take him up on it?"

"Nope. According to Mario, she turned him down." Nicki paused for a moment. "And he also said that Catherine mentioned she was meeting someone later that evening. Someone who made her nervous."

"That could be why she acted so wonky with you and Rob," Jenna said.

"Mario thinks it was Charlie."

"Oh, good heavens no," Maxie instantly protested. "Charlie wouldn't hurt a fly."

Nicki knew that Charlie was a long-time friend of Maxie and her husband's. They considered the older, perennial bachelor part of their family, and he was always present in their home for every holiday and special event.

Nicki smiled at her. "I wouldn't think so either, but he *is* her boyfriend. At least he is according to Suzanne."

"I believe Charlie may have mentioned it," Maxie reluctantly conceded. "But if the person she was waiting for is the one who killed her, then it wasn't Charlie Freeman."

Jenna lifted her wine glass and looked at the others over its rim. "Well, if not Charlie the boyfriend, then who?"

CHAPTER ELEVEN

BY AN UNSPOKEN AGREEMENT, THEY ALL ATE IN RECORD TIME, startling Joe when they'd asked for the check less than thirty minutes after he'd delivered their order. After exiting the restaurant, they'd piled into Maxie's comfortable Mercedes and made the short drive back to Nicki's place, where Alex and Matt had left their cars.

Nicki had invited everyone in for a nightcap of their choice. Pleading a forty-minute drive home and an early start to her shift in the ER the following morning, Alex had declined and driven off after a flurry of quick goodbyes. Jenna also turned down the invitation, stating she still had work she wanted to complete on her preliminary plan for her newest client. Giving hugs all around, she strode off to her side of the townhouse, slamming the door loudly behind her.

Laughing over a habit that Jenna clearly had no inclination to change, Matt and Maxie followed Nicki up the walkway and through her front door. Both women retrieved their cell phones before dropping their purses onto the hallway table and heading to the kitchen. Nicki offered wine to her guests, but they chose sparkling water instead.

While Matt and Maxie talked over Mason's latest gardening project, Nicki only nodded occasionally as she took three bottles of Perrier out of the fridge and placed them on the counter. She remained silent even after she'd finished filling large tumblers with ice, content to stand on the opposite side of the large kitchen island and sip her water while she silently thought over everything they'd found out about Catherine.

"So. Are you going to let us in on it?"

Matt's question interrupted Nicki's train of thought and she wrinkled her nose when she glanced over at him. "Let you in on what?"

He moved his glass slightly to one side and leaned in, clasping his hands together on top of the counter. "On whatever it is that's going through that busy mind of yours."

"Yes, dear." Maxie nodded. "I do hope you're ready to talk. We're running out of polite conversation while you've been reasoning everything out."

"I haven't been able to figure out a reason for anything yet."

"My dear Sherlock," Matt began in the worst English accent Nicki had ever heard. "Talking things out usually brings clarity to any thought."

Maxie chuckled. "Did Dr. Watson say that?"

"No, he did not," Nicki declared. At Matt's raised eyebrow, she grinned. "English Lit minor, and I read every one of Sir Arthur Conan Doyle's Sherlock Holmes stories. Even *The Adventure of the Final Problem,* as painful as that was."

Matt frowned. "Why was that one painful?"

Nicki stared at him as if he'd grown two heads. "Because the author killed Sherlock off in that one." She cocked her head to one side and narrowed her eyes. "Don't tell me you've never read a Sherlock Holmes book?"

When Matt shook his head, Nicki made a mournful sound in her throat. "You're really missing out, Dillon. And what kind of Dr. Watson wanna-be has never read any of Sherlock's adventures?"

"I've never had the time. But if I keep getting cast in the role as your sidekick to murder investigations, maybe I'll pick one up."

"I guess this means you did not spend any time in an English Lit class?" Nicki teased, then waited through a full five seconds of Matt's silence before sending Maxie an amused look.

The older woman threw up her hands. "Oh for goodness' sake, Mathew Dillon. That was your very obvious opening to tell Nicki what you *did* major in." She shook her head at him. "He majored in engineering." Maxie reached over and gave Matt's folded hand a gentle pat. "See, dear? That wasn't so hard."

"Thank you for letting me know that little tidbit about you," Nicki said to Matt with a perfectly straight face. While a streak of red visibly crept up the stubbornly silent Matt's neck, Nicki gave Maxie a curious look. "I've always wondered why you know so much about Matt?"

"Oh, well now. That's something we should discuss in private. Would tomorrow morning be convenient?" She winked at Nicki when Matt groaned out loud.

Sitting up until his back was ramrod straight, he glanced between the two women. "Matt, who I'd like to point out is sitting right here, would like to get back to the discussion about murder." He fixed a stare on Nicki, his brown eyes softening behind the lenses of his heavily rimmed glasses. "You were saying that you haven't been able to figure something out?"

"Quite a few things, actually." She tore her gaze away from Matt's so she could concentrate enough to mentally arrange the most puzzling points. Sometimes her editor did have an odd effect on her. "The chief said nothing had been taken from Catherine's house. Not even her money or credit cards. So the motive wasn't a robbery."

"Unless, like the chief said, you and your date suddenly showing up scared him off," Matt pointed out.

"But if someone had run away, where would they have run to? The house isn't that big. We'd have heard him going through the kitchen and out the back door. It only took us a minute to find

Catherine's body, so the only way someone could have gotten out without us seeing him would have been to leave very quickly, and I'm sure he would have made some noise."

"He or she, dear," Maxie gave a dramatic sigh when Nicki looked over at her. "While we were strolling past the grapes immortalized in bronze, Alex was proclaiming that we should definitely include Suzanne on the suspect list."

"She kept referring to her as 'interviewed person number one', in case anyone happened to overhear us." Matt grinned when Nicki laughed.

She could just imagine Alex putting on her best doctor voice and listing all the reasons why "interviewed person number one" should be a prime suspect. Not to mention Maxie's horrified reaction at the thought of one member of her cherished Society killing off another.

"She mentioned the very same thing to me as we were driving away after our talk with Suzanne. But as a full-fledged member of our group, Alex can add anyone she thinks has a reason to want Catherine dead to the suspect list on our murder board."

"I didn't catch the reason Alex was so sure that Suzanne should be a suspect?" Matt asked. "And she was pretty adamant about it."

Nicki schooled her features into a sober look to keep from laughing again. She didn't want to upset Maxie. "Alex is convinced Suzanne has an obsessive personality and is crazy."

"Of course she isn't anything of the sort," Maxie instantly declared. "She and Catherine were just very close, is all. And I'm sure this gourmet cooking phase of hers, and her choice of hairstyle and clothing, is simply a coincidence."

Matt's gaze flicked between the two women. "What's going on with this Suzanne?"

"It's a long story, and one of Alex's stranger theories," Nicki said. "We should get back to the murder."

Matt shrugged. "No problem. I'll just call Alex and ask her. Or maybe I'll ask Ty." He shrugged again when Nicki put her hands on her hips and gave him a hard stare. "So back to the murder. Let's assume you would have heard some person, male or female, running off. Since you didn't, what does that leave?"

"If she wasn't being robbed, then someone had another motive," Maxie offered.

"Someone she knew." When Matt and her landlady gave her a startled looked, Nicki nodded back at them. "Why else would she let someone get behind her unless she knew them and was comfortable? If it had been a stranger, she probably would have turned her head at least to keep them in sight and then have had a defensive wound of some kind. At least I didn't see one." Nicki chewed on her lower lip, thinking through the crime scene. "But if it *was* someone she knew, why was there only one place setting? Even if they'd dropped in unexpectedly, Catherine would have invited them to share her meal. And if she'd been expecting someone, like Mario said, it must have been for a time after her shift because, once again, there was only one place setting."

Matt tipped his head back and closed his eyes. "Maybe someone did drop by unexpectedly, and they started arguing and it got out of hand?"

"If that's the case, we should talk to Beatrice," Maxie said.

Matt opened his eyes and turned his head to look at her. "Who's Beatrice?"

"Beatrice Riley, the neighbor across the street from Catherine. You'll never meet a bigger busybody. But if anyone ran out of that house, or went in and then had an argument with Catherine, Beatrice would know. She thinks it's her duty to keep a close watch on everything and everyone from that big picture window in her front room." Maxie raised her gaze to the ceiling. "I've known Beatrice for over two decades. MyMason and I had the unfortunate experience of living next door to her after we were first married. That was before we bought this property. She's one of the reasons we decided to build a house where we'd have no neighbors around us."

Matt grinned at Nicki. "Since Mario was interview subject number two, Beatrice Riley sounds like the perfect person to be interview subject number three. She'll help you hone your skills."

Nicki ignored him and went back to concentrating on the puzzle. Why did Catherine go home, only to eat food from the restaurant she'd just left? And if she'd only been on her shift for an hour or so before taking that early dinner break, so why go into work at all? Why didn't she simply offer to start the hostess job after whatever it was she'd needed to have an early dinner break for? Her brow wrinkled in confusion, Nicki relayed her thoughts to her guests. It didn't take long for them to look as puzzled as she felt.

"Maybe after the divorce she was at loose ends," Maxie said slowly. "Any excuse to get out of the house and among other people, even for an hour or so, might have been welcome under her current circumstances. With her daughter living elsewhere, this might have been the first time Catherine had ever lived alone, and she was still getting used to it."

Nicki considered that. It sounded like a plausible explanation, but she wasn't sure because she'd never really lived alone. She'd gone from her mother's apartment to sharing one with Alex and Jenna. And even now, while technically she lived alone, she and Jenna literally shared a wall. Nicki glanced over at Matt. "You live alone. Do you ever have a burning need to get out among people?"

Matt scratched the side of his neck as he blinked and scrunched his mouth up. "It's different for guys. When we want company, we're not usually thinking of 'people' but of hot women." He sent a sheepish look to Maxie. "I'm sorry. I shouldn't have said that."

Maxie waved him off. "It's all right, dear. Men thought the same thing when I was your age. But Catherine was a little older, so I'm assuming her thoughts weren't always turned to the bedroom."

"Yes, well, let's move on," Nicki declared. "Since the chief took Ramona through the house, I gather Catherine's daughter is in town. I wonder if she just arrived, or was here when her mother was murdered?"

"Which might make her as prime a suspect as Suzanne," Matt said.

"According to Suzanne, she would be. She'd asked her mother for more money to continue her education abroad, and Suzanne told us that Catherine had turned her down. Apparently there's a trust from Ramona's father, which Catherine had full control of."

"That's right," Maxie nodded. "Until Ramona's thirtieth birthday, which won't come around for another four years or so." She smiled at the questioning glance from Nicki. "Catherine told me that some time ago."

"Which will make her interview person number four, since I'm assuming she'll at least stay in town until there's some sort of memorial service," Matt said. "Is there a candidate for interview subject number five?"

"The ex-husband, of course," Maxie and Nicki said together.

Matt shook his head. "When it comes to murder, it really doesn't pay to be an ex-husband. You almost have to start out proving you didn't do it."

"And the twin sister," Nicki added.

Matt sat up straighter and adjusted his glasses on his nose. "Our victim had a twin sister?"

"Yes, but she lives thirty minutes away, in Sonoma. Her name's Cynthia." Maxie smiled when Matt yawned. Her blue eyes crinkled at the corners when she glanced over at Nicki. "Between the time change and all the running around with us today, I think your potential boyfriend is about to fall asleep right where he's sitting."

"Maxie," Nicki warned. She smiled at Matt. "She's right though. You look beat. Will you be okay to drive back to your hotel?"

"It's only fifteen minutes from here. I can make it just fine." Matt stood and stretched to his full six feet. Looking at him from her much more diminutive stature, Nicki tried not to think about the fact that unlike Rob, Matt didn't need lifts in his shoes in order to reach that height. But then again, she doubted if he'd use lifts in his shoes even if he was a half-foot shorter. Matt was too comfortable with himself to worry about measuring up to someone else's opinion about his looks. She really did like that about him.

"What's our plan for tomorrow?"

"Plan?" Nicki repeated, her mind suddenly blank.

Matt snapped his fingers in the air. "Hello. Earth to Nicki. Where did you go?"

"Nowhere. I was just formulating the plan." She certainly wasn't going to admit out loud that she'd been comparing Rob to one of Matt's finer points. And her editor did have a few in his favor.

"Tomorrow, Nicki?" Matt prompted.

"Yes. Tomorrow. I thought I'd go out and talk to a suspect who wasn't on your list. Charlie Freeman."

"The boyfriend?" Matt slapped an open palm against his forehead. "I *must* be tired. He should have been first on the list."

"Except he'd never hurt anyone like that," Maxie insisted, once again coming to Charlie's defense.

"We just need to find out the same things the chief knows, since I'm sure he's already talked to Charlie," Nicki assured her.

"That's a certainty." Matt offered his arm to Maxie. "Can I escort you out to your car? It's time we left Nicki to experience some of that 'living alone solitude' she's missed out on."

Maxie bowed her head before slipping one arm through his. "I have an appointment in the morning, and Jenna will most likely still be busy with her project, so I'm assuming you'll be going along to look after our Nicki when she goes to talk with Charlie?"

"That's also a certainty," Matt replied as the two of them started to stroll off.

"Excuse me," Nicki called after them. "Nicki grew up in New York City, so I'm pretty sure she can look after herself."

"Be sure to bring your laptop when you pick me up tomorrow, Miss Connors," Matt said over his shoulder. "Maybe we can also get some work done at those other jobs of ours. You do remember them, don't you? The ones that pay the bills."

CHAPTER TWELVE

NICKI AND MATT PULLED UP TO THE FRONT OF THE PARKING lot at Charlie's winery. Matt had to give the passenger door several hard pushes before it finally opened and he could unfold himself from the narrow bucket seat. Nicki had been grateful when he hadn't said one word when the car had refused to start for several minutes after they'd stopped for coffee at Starbucks. Or when it had stalled at a stop sign about a mile from their destination. She really didn't want to get into a discussion on why her budget wouldn't stretch to a car payment quite yet. But she had high hopes for sometime next year. Of course it would have to be another used car, but that was okay. As long as it had less than two hundred thousand miles on it, she would be better off than she was now.

WineTime, the winery Charlie had owned for well over a decade, boasted a gorgeous tasting room, with huge windows offering panoramic views of the meticulously landscaped grounds, which showcased dozens of rose bushes bursting with red and white flowers. A bubbling brook wound its way under a small bridge leading to the front door.

Inside, more flowers adorned high tables that were surrounded with tall stools, and a highly polished wine bar curved around two sides of the room. The view out the large picture windows was relaxing, the room truly lovely, and the small bites from the winery's kitchen were delicious.

But the wine was simply awful.

Nicki grinned. Despite that fact, the tasting room did a fair business. Mostly from the locals who simply liked Charlie and enjoyed the atmosphere, the view and the food. Everyone who came purchased a tasting flight or at least one glass of wine. And if Charlie was making his rounds in the tasting room, they even drank it. Otherwise it was bought and then left untouched.

"Does Charlie know we're coming?" Matt looked around, his gaze lingering on the view. "I'm looking forward to meeting him."

"And tasting his wine?" Nicki smiled and waved at an older gentleman who'd been talking to the barman when they'd come in, but was now making his way across the floor.

"Looking forward to it." Matt turned toward Charlie who'd stopped in front of Nicki.

Reaching out long arms, the winery owner gave her a hug. Almost as tall as Matt, and slightly hunched in the shoulders, Charlie looked like a softer version of Clint Eastwood in his older years. Although his personality was certainly far different. Charlie was not only trusting and very open about himself, but also exceedingly polite, with an old-world manner and charm about him. Nicki was still having a hard time picturing the fast-paced, high-fashion Catherine as being any kind of romantic match with Charlie.

She returned his hug then stepped back and nodded at Matt. "This is my friend, Matt Dillon. He's also the editor and owner of *Food & Wine Online.*

Charlie shook Matt's hand, a vague smile on his lips. "Do you own that internet magazine that gave a nice write-up about my winery?"

Matt grinned. "Nicki did the write-up, the magazine only published it."

"She's a nice girl," Charlie beamed. "Smart and pretty, too. Have you noticed that?"

Matt grinned when Nicki gave him an exaggerated blink of her eyes. "I have."

"Matt's looking forward to trying your wine." Nicki didn't dare look at Matt when she made that announcement.

"Wonderful. I'd be happy to buy you a glass. Our pink Chablis is very good this year." Charlie raised his hand to signal the barman, lifting one finger and pointing at Matt before giving a questioning look to Nicki.

Catching it, Matt's grin grew wider. "I'm sure Nicki would like to have a glass."

"I'm driving, so no, I can't," Nicki quickly countered.

"Not even a short pour? I'm sure that's under the legal limit," Matt said.

"Better safe than sorry, I always say." Nicki turned her brightest smile on Charlie. "I hope you have some time to sit with us for a few minutes. I thought you might need to talk about Catherine."

"I've already spent several hours with Suzanne, so I'm pretty much talked out about all of Catherine's wonderful qualities. But I'd be happy to answer any questions you might have, and tell you the same things I told the chief." He gave Nicki a wink. "My good friend, Maxie, called this morning and said you'd be by since you were investigating the case. Just like you did with that winemaker over at Holland's who got himself killed. I'm glad you're on the case. I told that to Maxie too. And I think the chief could use the help. There's only him, Danny and Fran down at that station."

Charlie gestured to the empty table directly behind them, and they all settled onto tall stools. Tim came over with a single glass of wine and set it down in front of Matt. Nicki and Charlie both watched as he took his first sip.

"Good, isn't it?" Charlie boomed out as Nicki quickly raised a hand to cover her smile.

Her eyes sparkled as she watched Matt fight not to make a face. She also had to hand him the 'good sport' award when he raised his glass and took another sip.

"Thank you for the wine. I always appreciate a good wine." Matt said diplomatically, even as he pressed the side of his leg firmly against Nicki's.

She took it as a warning not to laugh. She'd never hurt Charlie's feelings that way, but had to admit that watching Matt choke down the worst wine in America, it was a close thing.

"Now that we have the tasting out of the way, go ahead and ask your questions."

"Were you supposed to meet Catherine that night?" Having no idea just how deeply involved Charlie and Catherine were, Nicki intended to do her very best not to use the words "killed" or "murdered" in the same breath as Catherine's name.

"Yes. I was going to have dinner at Mario's and then go to her place afterwards. I told the chief the same thing."

"Then you were going to walk home with her after her shift?"

Charlie scratched his head. "The chief asked the same thing, but I didn't know she was working at Mario's that night. She didn't say so. She didn't mention to me about having another appointment before she'd be free to get together, and she didn't say anything about filling in as hostess at Mario's either. Chief Turnlow told me her appointment had been canceled. Maybe that's why she decided to go to Mario's thinking we could meet there. She could work a little while I was having my dinner."

"So you were never going to Catherine's for dinner?" Matt asked.

Charlie shifted his gaze to the tall editor. "Nope. Catherine couldn't cook and didn't want to learn either. We always went out. Or ate here." Charlie's eyes narrowed into a squint as he stared at Matt. "Say. Did anyone ever tell you that you look a bit like that cartoon fellow? I think his name is Waldo?"

"Once or twice."

Again Nicki had to give Matt some 'good sport' points for

keeping a smile on his face after being asked the same question for what she was sure was the millionth time.

"I didn't realize you had dinner at Mario's. You must have come in after we'd left," Nicki drew Charlie's attention away from Matt before the older man could ask any more Waldo questions.

Charlie shook his head. "I didn't. I got so involved with working on my roses, that I just plain forgot."

"Do you like to garden the way Maxie's husband does?" Nicki smiled at the thought of the two men pruning rose bushes together.

The winery owner chuckled at that. "No, no. He does landscaping. I prefer to create and grow new flowers. I have a greenhouse right in back of the tasting room. I spend the better part of almost every day in there. Growing roses is really my first love. I'm actually not all that fond of making wine, but roses won't get me a free invitation to all the private wine tasting events in the area, and my wine will. So I just keep on making it, and folks keep on trying it. I guess that's all that really matters." He glanced over at Matt. "I'm getting on in years though, so I'm thinking I might hire a manager for the winery. You wouldn't happen to be looking for a new job now, would you?"

"No, sir, I'm not. Sorry." Matt adjusted his glasses and his tone turned serious. "Was anyone here that night who saw you working in the greenhouse?"

"No. We close the tasting room at five and all the winery workers go home about then too. I puttered around until ten or so, and then came in and watched the news and went to bed. Didn't think about meeting Catherine until the next day when Suzanne called me with the bad news." Charlie gazed out the big window for a long moment. "Didn't quite know what to do with myself after that call. This is the first time I've been in the tasting room since I spoke with Suzanne, and I haven't set a foot in the greenhouse." He turned back to Nicki with a sad smile. "Told all this to the chief, too."

"When was the chief here?" It worried Nicki that Charlie didn't have an alibi.

"Yesterday afternoon, around lunchtime." Charlie pulled out a small notebook from the pocket of his shirt and glanced at the scribbles on the front page. "He called this morning and said he wanted me to come down to the station. I guess they found lots of fingerprints, and he needs mine so he can eliminate those."

Or use them as evidence against you, Nicki thought. She sent a worried look to Matt who sent one right back to her.

Completely oblivious to their silent communication, Charlie chuckled quietly. "It's kind of exciting in a strange way. I've never been close to a murder investigation before."

Nicki sincerely hoped that having his fingerprints eliminated was as close as the chief intended to have Charlie get to Catherine's murder. But a sinking feeling in the pit of her stomach was telling her something else.

Sighing, she placed a gentle hand on Charlie's arm. "Did Catherine happen to mention to you who she had an appointment with that day? The one the chief said was canceled."

"She said Cynthia. I thought she meant her sister, but it could have been someone else with that name." He hung his head a little lower. "I wasn't paying much attention."

"That's okay. We'll find out." Nicki hesitated a moment, not sure what Matt would think of her next question, but hoped he'd go along with her plan. "If you're going to go see the chief, I'd love to ride with you. I need to stop in to see him too." She glanced over at Matt who raised a questioning eyebrow at her. "Matt can drive my car back and I can meet him at the hotel. We have some work we need to get done."

Charlie nodded and smiled. "I'd be happy to give you a ride, if you're okay to let Matt drive your car. Some people are touchy about that."

"Oh, not me." She turned toward Matt. "How about it? Think you can handle my car after that beautiful new BMW you have in your garage at home?"

"Su-re." Matt conveyed his feelings about Nicki's Toyota by drawing the one word out until it was almost two syllables.

"Just let me get my keys and I'll meet you in the parking lot out front." Charlie hopped off his stool and walked to the back of the room while Nicki and Matt went out the front door.

As they approached the sad-looking Toyota with its faded blue paint, Matt rattled the keys in his hand while he gave it a hard stare. "I gather you have some kind of roadside assistance service around here."

"The garage in town. Ask for Don, and be sure to tell him it's about Nicki's car."

Matt leaned a hip against one fender and crossed his arms over his chest. "I think your car is sending you some kind of message when you have roadside assistance on speed dial. How many times have you had to call for this guy's help?"

"I've lost count," Nicki admitted. "But he always comes as soon as he can." She laughed. "He's more reliable than the car."

"That's great. Just what I need to worry about. Your car breaking down in the middle of nowhere late at night."

Thinking maybe he was right, and she wasn't being fair to him, Nicki held out her hand. "I can drive, Matt, and you go with Charlie to see the chief. I'll be right behind you."

Matt held the keys further away from her. "I'm not having you drive this thing any more than you need to until we can get you better transportation."

"I already have that planned out. Now give me my keys."

"Planned out for when?" Matt's voice held a skeptical note, and he snorted when she said, "next spring".

Shaking his head, he unlocked the car and folded himself into the driver's seat. After he'd adjusted the setting to accommodate his much longer legs, Matt closed his eyes and turned the key. Nicki was surprised right along with him when the engine easily turned over. Rolling his eyes at her smug smile, Matt backed the car out of the parking space just as Charlie pulled up in his older, but beautifully kept, Mercedes. As she slid into the leather seat, Nicki waved at Matt who immediately put her car into gear and puttered off toward the highway leading back into town.

CHAPTER THIRTEEN

NICKI WALKED INTO HER TOWNHOUSE EARLY THAT EVENING AND straight back to her kitchen. Her trip with Charlie to see Chief Turnlow hadn't left her with a warm and fuzzy feeling. Instead, cold chills had run up her back as she'd watched Danny fingerprint the nice older gentleman, and the chief go over his explanation of his whereabouts the night his girlfriend was killed. Even Matt hadn't been able to cheer her up much, although working side-by-side with him on several articles for background pieces on the upcoming Los Angeles Food & Wine Festival had been a pleasant distraction from her worries over Charlie.

Matt had stayed behind at the hotel to finish up the work, but only after she'd sworn to him at least three times that she was going straight home, and had no intention of straying outside for the rest of the evening. And if she did, she would call him. If her car broke down on the way home, she would call him. She even added in that if she ran out of milk, she would call him. At that point he'd just glared at her as she'd given him a quick airy wave and made a dash for the hotel door.

Standing at her kitchen counter she pulled out a bottle of the Grand Reserve Chardonnay from Holland winery. It had been a gift from the owner for identifying the person responsible for killing his head winemaker. Giving herself a healthy pour, she took her glass into her home office and sat in her desk chair, staring at her murder board. She told herself she would spend a few minutes updating it, and then put it aside for the evening and work on the outline for her next spy novel. She was sure her hero, Tyrone Blackstone, was feeling very neglected by now.

The sound of the front door opening was followed by Jenna's distinct "helloooo". Nicki waited until after the inevitable door-slamming before she called back.

"In the office." When Jenna's face appeared around the corner, Nicki lifted her glass. "It's the Grand Reserve from Holland's. If you want some, the bottle is in the wine fridge, bottom shelf."

Jenna came in and plopped down on the small sofa and held up the long-necked bottle in her hand. "As it so happens, I was in the mood for a beer. Since I know you don't stock that particular item, I brought my own."

Nicki leaned back in her desk chair and took a leisurely sip of her wine. "So, how's the plan going for the new client? Hit any glitches that will require you to make a trip to Silicon Valley?" The only thing Nicki knew about Trident Industries was that it was headquartered in Silicon Valley. And its founder was in his mid-thirties, very easy to look at, and very wealthy thanks to being an engineering genius when it came to designing computer programs.

"Hard to have a glitch when I'm figuring out how to best show-case the coolest software in the world. Did you know one of their product lines is only sold to law enforcement agencies? Oh. And the CIA. I'm not sure if they qualify as 'law enforcement', but they're some sort of agency." Jenna's eyes shone behind her glasses. "Their age and face enhancement programs are far superior to anything else I've ever seen. And they have a fingerprint scanner that can be installed in all kinds of portable devices." Jenna paused and sighed. "When I grow up, I so want to be like the guy who designed this stuff."

Nicki laughed. "From what I read of your new client's profile, he's only five years older than you are."

"Then I've got a long way to go in a short amount of time. But before that, I'm supposed to tell you that Alex wants a 'catch-up' call in..." Jenna glanced at her wristwatch. "Oh, about three minutes."

"That's perfect." Nicki immediately perked up a bit. Talking this whole thing over with her friends was just what was needed. The well-grounded Alex and the ever-logical Jenna, would help her unravel this puzzle. Nicki was sure of it. Opening her desk drawer, she removed the power cord for her phone and plugged it into the wall. She was just setting it on its stand when it rang. Nicki pressed the answer button and grinned at Jenna who'd moved and was now sitting on the floor next to Nicki.

"Hey, Alex! How's the doctoring world?"

"Same as usual. Lives are saved, people go home happy." The background noise from the call sounded as if Alex was taking a brisk walk.

"Where are you?" Jenna demanded. "It sounds like you're passing through Grand Central Station."

"The ER is packed tonight. I'm just going through the lobby to get to a quieter place outside. There isn't one peaceful spot inside at the moment."

"Well walk faster," Jenna complained.

"Ha ha. Now stop talking, I told the staff I'd only take a twenty-minute lunch break tonight."

The noise level coming through the phone suddenly dropped to near silence. Nicki guessed Alex had finally made it outside and was headed to that quiet place she knew about.

"Okay. I wanted some privacy as well as quiet, "Alex explained. "Are you near the murder board?"

"We're in my office," Nicki confirmed.

"Good. Then you can update the board as we go along. I have the information from the autopsy report."

Jenna sat straight up and pumped a fist. "Way to go Alex! How did you get that?"

"The Chief of Staff in the emergency department is friends with Dr. Thomas Garland. He's the medical examiner for the county. The chief was kind enough to cash in a favor and got the information from Dr. Tom."

"And what did you have to promise your chief in return?" Nicki was sure the information hadn't come without some kind of price tag on it.

"I have to spend some of my days off helping Dr. Tom in the ME's office, and I have to work Halloween," Alex admitted. "My Chief of Staff can't find anyone to cover for him since he's on the rotation that night, and he wants to be sure he's home so his teenagers will behave."

"He's dreaming," Jenna called out from her place by the board, the marker poised in her hand. "So what do you have?"

"Believe me, this is fresh off the press." Alex's voice dropped. "I don't even think the police chief has it yet, since Dr. Tom was reading off his notes."

Nicki leaned forward, eager to hear what Alex had to say. She'd definitely be baking lemon bars later on. They were a particular favorite of Alex's. And an apple spice cake for her to take to Dr. Tom when Alex put in her day with the ME. Maybe if he knew how delicious the bribes could be, they'd have a friend in the coroner's office. *Not that we'll need one, since this can't possibly happen again. But just in case.*

"The official cause of death is from a stab wound," Alex began, then paused. Nicki could hear the crackle of paper through the phone.

"If that's it, you definitely got gypped, and I wouldn't do the Halloween gig," Jenna yelled from across the room.

"There's more. I just need to get these notes in order. Okay. Here we go. She had a small last meal of some pasta, seafood and bread."

"The rest of it was still on her plate and splattered across the tablecloth," Nicki confirmed.

There were more sounds of paper being shuffled before Alex picked up her narrative again. "According to Dr. Tom, there wasn't anything unusual in her blood work, and it didn't show that she'd consumed any alcohol in the hours before her death. She was in reasonably good shape, and I quote the doctor here, 'for a woman her age'."

Nicki shook her head. "I hope he doesn't put that in the official report, because that's just mean."

"I second that," Jenna said.

"Let's see. Time of death was approximately two hours before you found her, Nicki. Now let's see. He also related some of the forensic findings." There was another pause and more shuffling sounds. "There were two stab wounds, I won't tell you where exactly, but both entered through her back, and both hit vital organs, so she would have bled out in just a minute or two. The knife penetrated just under six inches."

Nicki thought that over as Jenna's marker made squeaking noises across the board. "I could still see part of the blade, so the knife must have been longer than six inches, and from the handle, it looked like it was from one of Zelite's lines."

"And give a gold star to the gourmet chef. It was a ten-inch, Zelite chef's knife. And very sharp according to Dr. Tom. Is that significant?"

"That's a high-end and expensive knife for someone who refuses to cook at all." Nicki tilted her head back and closed her eyes. Why would Catherine have a knife like that in her kitchen? Assuming, of course, it came from Catherine's kitchen.

She sighed out loud. This case was getting more and more confusing everywhere she looked. "I don't suppose there were any fingerprints on it?" Nicki doubted it, but she had to ask.

"Not a one."

"So whoever stabbed Catherine wasn't strong enough to shove the knife all the way in." Nicki's forehead wrinkled in thought.

"Or knew he didn't have to in order to cause enough damage to kill her. Especially with two wounds," Alex pointed out. "Maybe the knife wasn't Catherine's? Maybe the killer brought it with him or her?"

"So someone she knows shows up at the door with a ten-inch chef's knife in his hand and says what?" Jenna asked. "I just brought this along in case you needed me to cut something up?" She scoffed. "I vote that it was already there."

"It does sound more logical," Alex agreed. "Someone carrying around a knife with a ten-inch blade is bound to be noticed."

"But it doesn't fit Catherine's personality at all," Nicki argued. "A high-end chef's knife owned by someone who doesn't cook?"

"Well, run it by Matt in the morning. Maybe he'll have a fresh idea," Alex said. "And speaking of Matt..."

"I don't think we were speaking about Matt." Nicki gave Jenna a wary glance as her friend snapped on the top of the marker and walked back toward the desk, propping one hip on its edge.

"I'd like to talk about Matt." Jenna grinned.

"I second that," Alex said. "You're outvoted, Nicki."

She lifted her hands in an 'I-don't-care' gesture. "It's going to be a short conversation then, since there isn't anything to talk about. But I wish you'd stop teasing him about the boyfriend wannabe thing. He gets really embarrassed every time either of you brings it up."

"We didn't bring it up, Maxie did," Jenna pointed out. "And he was only embarrassed because it was true."

"You should have seen him when we took our walk through the square." Alex jumped in before Nicki could get out a protest. "When Maxie told him that another guy had a head start on him, and he needed to stop stalling or Rob would sweep you off your feet, all Matt said was 'no comment'."

"Maxie might have been exaggerating just a tad," Jenna admitted. "We all know Rob can't stop talking about himself long enough to sweep you off your feet. And I guess we could have let Matt in on that, but we wanted to hear what he had to say."

"And he very politely said 'no comment'." Nicki firmly tamped down that twinge of disappointment. It certainly made his feelings clear enough to her. "He's a very nice guy. It would've been insulting if he'd told my landlady and two best friends that he's not interested, so he simply went with the kinder 'no comment'." She paused and took in a deep breath, ignoring the grin that appeared on Jenna's face. "Even if he can't sweep me off my feet, Rob is still my boyfriend."

Jenna shook her head. "No, he's not. Lover-boy is just a date whenever he's in town and you're free. By the way, have you talked to Rob lately?"

"He called this morning. He's in Atlanta on a last-minute business trip. He wanted to know if the chief had mentioned him having to come back to Soldoff for another interview, or for a trial."

"That's nice that he called." Alex's tone fairly dripped with sweetness. "Did he ask how you were holding up? And you don't have to make an excuse for him. I know he didn't."

"Wow. There's a shocker." Jenna crossed her arms and stared at her friend.

"Oh shoot. I have to start walking back." Alex said. "Did you find out anything from Catherine's boyfriend? I thought you were going to go talk to him today?"

"I did. Charlie is the sweetest man. He likes to grow roses, and like Maxie said, I can't see him hurting a fly much less stabbing Catherine in the back."

"Anything else?"

"Yes. He was supposed to meet Catherine at her house that night after he had dinner at Mario's. He didn't know she would be working there that evening. But he forgot and went to bed around ten o'clock. So he has no alibi."

"Uh oh. That's not good," Jenna said. "I like Charlie. Hate his wine, but like him. He wouldn't do something like this."

"I went with him today when he went to the police station to get his fingerprints matched to any that were found in Catherine's house. That was really an 'uh oh' moment, although he didn't seem to realize it."

Nicki frowned when a series of beeps emitted from her phone. "Another call is coming in."

"No problem," Alex said. "I have to get back to work. I'll talk to you this weekend when I come for a visit, with Tyler tagging along to act as our collective bodyguard to keep Matt happy. Bye."

With that connection broken, Nicki touched the 'answer' button that had popped up with the second call.

"Hello?"

"Nicki, it's Maxie. I can't talk long, dear, but I just got a call from Ramona. She wants us to meet her at Catherine's house, and go through all her mother's writing journals to see if there's anything worth publishing."

Nicki's eyebrows winged up in surprise. "Ramona? Catherine's daughter?"

"That's right, dear. I wanted to call you right away so you can get started on a delicious treat. Just in case we need a small bribe."

Nicki groaned. She hadn't planned on anything but a good night's sleep, not staying up late to make a dessert for Catherine's daughter.

"I'll pick you up about ten. And I'll call Matt at his hotel to let him know when to be ready since you won't have time with the baking you'll need to do between now and then."

When Nicki let out a second groan, Maxie laughed.

CHAPTER FOURTEEN

NICKI, MAXIE AND MATT WERE SITTING IN MAXIE'S CAR IN front of Catherine's cute Cape Cod-style house, staring at the steps leading up to the porch and front door.

Reaching over the back of Nicki's seat, Matt placed a hand on her shoulder. "Are you sure you want to go back in there? You can stay out here while Maxie and I talk with Catherine's daughter."

"I'll be fine. Suzanne told us Ramona was angry that her mother had refused to give her extra money from her father's trust, so she could spend a year studying abroad. I'd like to hear what her alibi is for the night Catherine was killed."

"I would like to hear that too," Maxie declared. "I'm hoping Charlie isn't the only one who doesn't have someone to vouch for his whereabouts that night."

The three of them fell silent again for a moment before Maxie straightened her shoulders and made a move to open the car door. "Well, there's no reason to put this off. She glanced at Matt through the rear-view mirror. "Matt, dear. It might be better if you stayed in the car. Ramona could be in a very fragile state, and an unfamiliar, good-looking man close by may keep her from talking as freely as she would if it was just female friends of her mother's."

"I don't know," Matt said slowly. "Everyone involved in this seems to have a strange side to them." He nodded back as Maxie continued to stare at him. "This Suzanne sounds like a nut case, and last night? Mario wasn't even aware he was crushing Nicki's hand. Even Charlie is odd in his own way. He can't possibly be so scattered that he doesn't know that the wine he's been making for a decade or so is almost undrinkable. Now we're about to meet a daughter who can't seem to pick a major long enough to graduate from college, and a sister who didn't have much contact with her own twin. If Suzanne's account is to be believed."

Maxie sighed. "All of that is true enough. And you haven't even mentioned Catherine's ex-husband, who owns art galleries in several cities and favors wearing capes."

"Capes? You mean like a superhero in the comics?" Matt put his fingers to his temples and gave them a good rub. "Seriously?"

Nicki pressed her lips together to keep from laughing. When the urge had passed, she twisted around in her front passenger seat and looked at Matt. "And you also haven't mentioned the ultra-busy-body neighbor, who even this minute is probably watching us from her living room window."

"Great."

"That's small-town life." Nicki grinned at him. "While we're talking with Ramona, why don't you go talk to Beatrice Riley? Find out if she saw anyone go in or come out of the house that night besides Catherine."

"If anyone would know, Beatrice would," Maxie mumbled.

Picking up the plate of brownies she'd been carrying in her lap, Nicki opened the car door. "Let's get going before we talk ourselves out of it."

Walking backwards she winked at Matt as he came around to stand by the front of the car. "If you see a serial killer coming up the walk, be sure to send us a text." She smiled when he shook his head at her as Maxie laughed.

———

"THIS IS MY AUNT CYNTHIA. I ASKED HER TO COME ALONG since she hadn't been here since mom died. Gives her some closure, you know?" Ramona looked around before turning her gaze back to Maxie. Other than saying an indifferent "hello", Ramona had completely ignored Nicki.

"So mom's journals and stuff are on the coffee table." She pointed to the low oak table in front of the sofa.

Maxie nodded but the polite smile on her lips didn't quite reach her eyes. Nicki wasn't too impressed with Ramona's attitude about her mother's death either. Showing a little remorse would have been nice to see.

To Nicki, Ramona's seemingly unemotional reaction to her mother's death was as jarring as her hair. The young woman's brown locks were highlighted with thin strips of green running down both sides. To Nicki's eye, it gave the appearance of moss, or some kind of mold, growing in her hair. But other than the difference in their choice of hairstyle and color, Ramona looked exactly like her mom, right down to her medium height, slender figure and the gray eyes staring back at Maxie.

"We can get to that in a moment, dear." Maxie gave the gentle rebuke as she extended her smile to Ramona's aunt who was standing silently next to her niece. "It's been a while, Cynthia. It's nice to see you again, although I wish it were under different circumstances."

Cynthia nodded before looking pointedly at Nicki. Maxie raised one eyebrow, but her smile didn't budge.

"I asked Nicki along today since she's a published author." Maxie smoothly offered the explanation, waiting a beat before adding, "I'm sure, being a former librarian, that you're familiar with her novels?"

Catherine's twin gave a short nod before finally looking over at Nicki and belatedly acknowledged her presence. "Spy novels, I believe?"

Her underlying tone told Nicki just how little Cynthia thought of "spy novels". But she really didn't care about Cynthia's low opinion of her books. She enjoyed writing about Tyrone Blackstone's international adventures, and her books helped pay the bills. That's all that mattered to her.

"Isn't that a new look for you, dear?"

Touché, Nicki thought, although she was polite enough to keep her grin to herself. Maxie's tone made it clear what she thought about the clearly dyed, black hair that was chopped off into a ragged pixie cut. It had a punk-lifestyle look to it that was completely at odds with the prim white blouse and matching sweater over dark blue pants and sensible, thick-soled shoes. Except for the same height and build as her sister, no one would ever mistake the fashionable Catherine and odd-looking Cynthia as twins.

"Her hair turned out great, didn't it?" Ramona didn't even glance at her aunt as she said it. "It turned out to be a good thing when that stupid Mira at her beauty shop ruined the mousy-brown color and deadly dull cut Aunt Cynthia had kept for years. This new cut is much more in tune with today's dark vibe."

Nicki at least agreed it gave off a dark vibe. Whether it was great or not, was a matter of opinion. But on Cynthia Dunton, it looked like it was at war with the rest of her.

"Your mother didn't care for it," Cynthia said. "And I have to agree with her. But it was the best that could be done under the circumstances."

"Yes, well, sometimes we just have to march on," Maxie said. "Why don't we sit down and go over your mother's writing? Maybe Nicki and Cynthia could get us something to drink. I'd like coffee, if there's any available. No cream or sugar. If there isn't any, a glass of ice water will be fine as well." She gave a brief wave toward the kitchen before latching onto Ramona's arm and propelling her toward the sofa.

"I'd be happy to help," Nicki was quick to offer, since she wanted to have a look in the kitchen.

Cynthia didn't say a word. She simply turned and walked toward the arched opening into the dining room.

Nicki followed, taking as much of a look around the room where Catherine had been murdered as she could before she stepped through the doorway leading into the kitchen. It was a reasonably sized space. Not quite as large as Nicki's, but large enough to accommodate three or four people during a meal preparation. Cynthia headed straight for the coffee maker, one of the few appliances out on the otherwise starkly clean and unadorned counters. Nicki came up beside her and discreetly began to open the drawers under the countertop on her right.

"Are you thinking Catherine kept her coffee cups in the drawers?" Cynthia's gaze remained on the pot she was filling from the faucet hanging over the farmhouse sink. Nicki tried not to wince as the former librarian used tap water for coffee. "Of course not. Unlike Maxie, I prefer sugar in my coffee."

"So you think she kept her sugar bowl in the drawers?"

"Maybe sugar packets." Nicki managed to keep her voice pleasant despite the hostility in Cynthia's tone. "Or a spoon to stir the coffee?"

Catherine's twin turned to face Nicki, the coffeepot gripped tight in one hand. "I may not be as glamorous or famous as you or Maxie Edwards, but I'm not stupid either. What are you looking for?"

Nicki met the bald, direct question in the same manner. "For the knife drawer. I don't see a butcher block with a set out on the counter, so I'm assuming Catherine kept all her knives in a drawer."

The older woman pointed to a drawer on the other side of the sink. "She kept them in there. And when you're finished looking, feel free to snoop around anywhere else in the kitchen."

Ignoring the sarcasm, Nicki forced out a sunny smile and a "thanks" before she stepped around Cynthia and opened the drawer that contained the knives. She sifted through them, looking for another Zelite knife. But no luck. She carefully ran a thumb across several of the blades before she closed the drawer.

Deciding she couldn't possibly sink any lower in Cynthia's

opinion, Nicki stepped over to the small built-in desk next to the door leading to the outside patio. There were only a few papers on top, and the only one that caught her eye was a receipt from an auction house. The item listed was a Madame Alexander doll. Nicki had seen four of them in a glass-enclosed case in the corner of the living room. The amount paid wasn't excessive, so she set that aside and opened the only small drawer the desk had. All it contained were a few pens and pencils, a grocery list and a large sticky note pad. Sighing, Nicki closed the drawer and turned to face Cynthia, who was staring at her.

"Find what you were looking for?"

Nicki smiled and pointed to the tray sitting on the kitchen counter. "I see the coffee is ready. Can I carry it in for you?"

Cynthia didn't answer her but kept her stare fixed on Nicki's face. "Before you ask any prying questions that will upset my niece, I'll be happy to tell you the same thing we both told the police chief. I was home alone when Catherine was murdered, and my niece was alone in a friend's apartment as well. Neither one of us can account for our time during the murder, but then since neither one of us killed Catherine, we don't have to. And a little help with this tray would be nice."

Again Nicki ignored the hostility clearly ringing in Cynthia's voice. She walked over, picked up the tray, and without another word said between them, led the way back to the living room.

Maxie and Ramona were still occupying the sofa. Maxie was reading over a journal while Ramona sat watching her, her arms folded in front of her and a bored expression on her face. She looked up when Nicki and Cynthia came into the room.

"I guess you found everything okay." Ramona jerked her head toward Maxie. "She's still looking mom's stuff over." Her gaze shifted to her aunt. "She said it might take a while to get anything published, and even then, any money would go into the estate."

"Ramona is concerned that her education will be disrupted if she has to wait for the funds." Maxie closed the journal in her hands and set it on the far side of the table before moving the rest of the papers aside as well. "You can set the tray down right here, dear."

"I'm not that concerned. Aunt Cynthia showed me a copy of mom's will. She left her whole estate to me, and my aunt is the executor."

"Executrix," her aunt corrected before looking over at Nicki. "And to satisfy your curiosity, I had a copy of the will because Catherine insisted I have one. She put everything into a trust for her daughter to be overseen by me until Ramona turns thirty-five."

"Probably because dad's trust says until I turn thirty." Ramona stuck her lip out in a pout worthy of any toddler. "Doesn't seem fair. But at least Aunt Cyn can give me the money I need."

"To study abroad?" Maxie smiled when Ramona shot her a mutinous look. "Your mother told me you were interested in going to school in Europe for a year."

"I'll be travelling, but not studying. I'm going to take some time off from school." Ramona reached over and started to dump sugar into one of the coffee cups. "I don't know for how long yet. But I'm leaving right after the memorial service. Aunt Cyn said she'd give me the money."

"When is the memorial service?" Nicki asked.

"Mom's friend, Suzanne, is arranging it. She said she'll let me know, but promised it would be in a couple of days. A week at the latest. And then I'm gone." Ramona sat back, leaving the coffee cup on the table after she'd barely taken a sip.

Maxie shook her head. "That's a shame. The Ladies in Writing Society is planning on having a memorial lunch for your mother at our next meeting in a few weeks." She glanced over at Cynthia. "We'd hoped you'd both be able to attend."

Ramona looked away and shrugged. "I'll be in Paris by then."

CHAPTER FIFTEEN

NICKI AND MAXIE HAD LET THEMSELVES OUT OF THE HOUSE, leaving Ramona and her aunt sitting silently in the living room of Catherine's cottage. Halfway down the stone walkway, Maxie let out a heavy sigh.

"It's a sad thing when someone you know is mourned so little by the family."

Nicki glanced back over her shoulder toward the porch. Cynthia Dunton was standing in front of the living room window, looking out at them. "I think the daughter has her defenses solidly up, and is hurting more than she's letting on." She turned her gaze toward the car where Matt was leaning against the trunk, waiting for them. "But I'm surprised by Cynthia's reaction. Catherine was her twin."

"Who was her polar opposite, and according to what Suzanne told you, hung onto the purse strings," Maxie pointed out.

Matt grinned at the two women walking toward him. He ran a hand through his thick dark hair, leaving a strand of it sticking straight up. Seeing it, Nicki smiled. The picture he made reminded her of the first time she'd seen Matt during a Skype call, when both of them had been sitting under some kind of grade-school-hallway lighting with a beige wall in back of them. Nicki's was in the small apartment in San Francisco that she'd been living in at the time, and Matt's was behind his desk in his cramped office in Kansas City. That was almost three years ago.

Maxie was right. He'd needed to do something other than stand on the sidelines while they had talked to Ramona and Cynthia. If nothing else, to take his mind off his rumbling stomach. Nicki could hear it when they got closer. She guessed that half an English muffin and the quick cup of coffee he'd confessed to having for breakfast after a long night of working late, was wearing off. She was always amazed at the amount of food Matt could eat, and was certain that by now he was probably starving.

"Find out anything interesting?" He stuck his hands into the pockets of his jeans.

"There's not one other Zelite knife in Catherine's kitchen." Nicki settled herself next to Matt and mimicked his stance of leaning against the car trunk. "And Catherine left everything in a trust to her daughter, which Cynthia will control." She turned her head to look at Matt, her lips twitching up into a smile. "And neither of them have an alibi for the night of the murder."

"And neither of them seem too upset about Catherine's death," Maxie added with a sniff and a frown. "They're even allowing Suzanne to plan the memorial service. Oh, and Cynthia had a disaster at the hair salon, resulting in a cut and color that is most unfortunate."

"Beatrice Riley mentioned the same thing." When both women gave him a questioning look, Matt nodded. "She said Cynthia stopped by a week ago, to introduce herself and bring Mrs. Riley a plate of chocolate chip brownies." His eyes laughed at Nicki from behind the large lenses of his glasses. "She said they were the best brownies she'd ever had. That was right before she mentioned Cynthia's hair. Cynthia told her that some new person at her shop had simply ruined it so badly that she'd ended up with orange hair, and she was so embarrassed that she'd been forced to cover her head with a scarf."

"Something I would have continued to do rather than walk around with that shaggy look she has now." Maxie crossed her arms and tapped one foot. "I don't know who deserves to be shot more. The woman who turned her hair orange, or the one who fixed it."

Nicki bit her lip to keep from laughing. After all, such a hair disaster as Cynthia Dunton clearly experienced was no laughing matter.

"Did Mrs. Riley have any other tidbits of information?"

Matt leaned back a little more, raising his face to the sun as his stomach continued to grumble.

"Well, she recognized you as the person who solved that wine-maker's murder." He smiled at Nicki. "Her words, not mine. She also said she'd 'swear on a stack of Bible's to Chief Turnlow himself, that no one else came out of the house after she saw you and Rob go in, and she didn't see anyone go into the house all day, except for Catherine."

"And unless she's changed her habit, which is highly unlikely, she wasn't monitoring the street from five to six o'clock. That's when she makes her dinner and then watches the news." Maxie nodded at Nicki's raised eyebrow. "Everyone in the neighborhood knows Beatrice's schedule."

Matt straightened out his long frame and grinned at Maxie. "Beatrice has a whole list of who she called 'uppity people', and I'm afraid you were on it." He laughed at Maxie's snort. "And so were Catherine and Ramona. According to Mrs. Riley, neither of them so much as looked her way, not even when she was out on the porch. She thought Catherine wouldn't have been at all happy if she'd known that Beatrice had a key to her house. She said a tenant who lived there about five years ago gave it to her, to help water her plants when she was gone. The landlord has never changed those locks."

"A key?" Nicki pushed away from the car, her brow furrowed in thought. "Does she still have the key?"

"I asked her that very same question. She said she went and

checked the minute she heard someone had gone into Catherine's home and killed her. Beatrice said the key is right where she left it."

"Oh." Nicki deflated a bit. "I guess that would have been too easy."

"Uh huh." Matt put an arm around her shoulders. "And Beatrice Riley has heard all about your interrogation methods too. So she's expecting the same treatment."

Nicki wasn't too sure she liked the sound of that. "What has she heard?"

"That you bribe with treats, dear. It's all over town, of course." Maxie eyed the tall editor. "What did you promise Beatrice to get her to talk?"

"I told her Nicki could make just about anything she'd like, but that her raspberry tarts were really good. She said she'd be happy with those. And she'll be at the Ladies in Writing charity event on Saturday, so she can pick them up there."

When Nicki groaned and smacked him lightly on the arm, Matt took a quick step away from her. "What was that for?"

CHAPTER SIXTEEN

MAXIE SLID INTO THE DRIVER'S SEAT OF HER CAR AND SHUT THE door. She tapped her polished nails against the leather-covered steering wheel before she turned toward Nicki.

"Suzanne is doing the memorial service? I still can't believe that's what I heard Catherine's daughter say."

"That's what Beatrice said too," Matt volunteered from the back seat. "I think she called it ridiculous."

"Of course it is. What grown daughter can't be bothered to plan her own mother's memorial service," Maxie snapped. "And I didn't get so much as a text message from Suzanne about it."

Nicki's eyes opened wider as she stared back at Maxie. She'd only known the genealogist for two years, but in all that time she'd never heard Maxie raise her voice or show the tiniest sign of being angry. Maxie had proclaimed on more than one occasion, that any negative emotions were a waste of energy. And at her age, she didn't have that much to waste.

"I'm sure Suzanne only wants to help," Nicki ventured. "She and Catherine were very close friends."

"More like joined at the hip." Maxie put her foot, which was clad in a fashionable high-heeled sandal, onto the brake and pushed the start button for the engine. "So of course she'd want to be part of the memorial."

After she'd pulled out onto the street, Matt leaned forward and rested his arm on the edge of the front seat. "Then I don't understand why you have a problem with her planning the memorial service?"

"*I* don't have a problem with it. *We* have a problem, meaning the Ladies in Writing Society has one."

"How so?" Nicki asked.

Maxie turned off the square, away from Matt's hotel.

"Where are we going?" Matt pointed behind them. "The hotel is the other way."

"To Suzanne's of course. She simply isn't capable of planning a memorial and the Society's charity event at the same time. Especially since Catherine was the organized one of the two of them, and she was co-chair along with Suzanne."

Suddenly Maxie's concern became crystal clear to Nicki. The charity event, with baked goods, arts and crafts, and donated items for sale, along with several demonstrations in painting, ceramics and cooking, was scheduled for this Saturday, to coincide with the festival going on in town this coming weekend. And that was just three days away.

"With everything going on, I hadn't given it a thought, and if any other of the members were chairing it, I'm sure it would be just fine. But Suzanne gets flustered so easily, and I haven't received any progress reports from her in the last few days. I might have to reassign an emergency chairwoman to get us through this last push. Especially if Suzanne is going to be spending all her time planning Catherine's memorial." She pursed her lips. "Let me think."

"Maybe you could think while we stop at a drive-thru and grab a quick bite?" Matt asked.

"We can get something in town after we call on Suzanne. It will be my treat, dear."

Nicki grinned when Matt gave a huge sigh and plopped back

into his seat. She turned to wink at him just as he gave a clearly longing look at Eddie's Burger Diner as they whizzed past. With an air of nonchalance, she held up a paper bag she'd left on the floor next to the passenger seat and jiggled it.

Matt eyed the bag. "What's that?"

"Maybe some brownies that didn't quite make it onto the plate that I left with Ramona and her aunt." Nicki gave a startled yelp when a long arm flashed over the seat back and grabbed the bag right out of her hand.

"You'd better not be messing with me, Connors." He quickly unrolled the top of the bag. He looked up and gave her a huge smile.

"I'd never be that mean to you, Dillon."

"Eat fast, dear. We're almost there. And please do so quietly. I need to make a phone call."

Apparently taking Maxie at her word, Matt practically stuffed a whole brownie into his mouth. Nicki rolled her eyes at him as Maxie spoke with another member of the Society on her car phone, disconnecting with a smile just as they pulled up in front of Suzanne's house.

Matt was still chewing his second brownie when Suzanne answered her front door. She was wearing jeans and a paisley top in a unique pattern, with several shades of blue and an occasional pop of gold. *At least it doesn't look as if she's spent the entire morning crying,* Nicki thought.

"Hi." Suzanne's gaze went right to Matt. "I wasn't expecting anyone this morning.

"We won't stay long. I know how busy you are." Maxie cocked her head to one side and stared until Suzanne got the hint.

"Oh. Won't you come in? I'm not sure what's in the refrigerator, but I'm sure I can come up with some refreshment."

"No need. This is just a quick visit. We have several other stops to make today." Maxie put a hand on Matt's arm. "Of course you know Nicki from the Society. But have you ever met her good friend, Matt?"

"No, I haven't." Suzanne stepped forward, which put her barely a hand's width away from Matt. She turned her face to look up into his startled eyes. "Hi. I'm Suzanne. Nicki's friend. She's mentioned you to me quite a number of times. I'm very glad to meet you."

Taken aback by the woman's very unexpected and forward behavior, Nicki's mouth dropped open as Suzanne put a hand on Matt's chest.

"Suzanne." Maxie's voice was sharp enough to startle Suzanne into jumping back, putting more space between herself and a thoroughly red-faced Matt. "I believe you'll recall that I told you that Matt is interested in Nicki."

Nicki closed her eyes. Trust Maxie to be very honest and direct. But at least she'd prevented Suzanne from plastering herself against her defenseless editor.

Suzanne's eyebrows squished together as she glanced over at Nicki. "But you said that..."

"Anything is possible," Nicki cut in, circling a hand around Matt's wrist and pulling him to stand closer to her. He immediately put an arm around her shoulders.

"We aren't here to talk about budding romances," Maxie announced. "Now that all introductions have been made, shall we sit down and discuss the upcoming event?"

Suzanne nodded and led the way into the living room. She plopped into an antique-looking chair and crossed her arms.

"What event are you talking about?"

"We just came from a discussion with Ramona and her aunt. They mentioned you were planning Catherine's memorial service?" Maxie paused, waiting for Suzanne's nod. "Of course I wanted to let you know right away that anyone from the Society would be happy to help."

"Well, I'm not sure..." Suzanne glanced over at Nicki and Matt. "Maybe that would be fine."

"Anyone except Nicki," Maxie clarified. "She's busy helping the chief solve Catherine's murder. And she'll be giving several cooking demonstrations during our society's charity event this weekend."

While Maxie diplomatically explained to Suzanne why it would be too difficult for her to continue on and plan the charity event on her own, and that Addie Young, who Maxie had called from the car, would be taking over most of it, Matt leaned over close to Nicki's ear.

"Thanks for the rescue."

"Don't mention it."

"When did Maxie say you'll be giving those cooking demonstrations?"

Nicki smiled. "This weekend. And Maxie told me the response has been very positive, so we're hoping for a good-sized crowd."

"Damn, I'll be in L.A."

Unable to make out what he'd said, Nicki glanced up at him. He smiled at her and ran a single finger down one of her cheeks before he got to his feet.

"I'm sorry ladies," he said when Maxie and Suzanne stopped their conversation to look at him. "But I need to step outside. I have a few business calls to make."

———

It took another twenty minutes of placating Suzanne before Nicki and Maxie could join Matt outside. The three of them walked to the car, with all of them shaking their heads.

Once they were on their way, Matt tapped Nicki on the shoulder. "You know she has your haircut. And I'm sure I've seen you in that shirt she was wearing."

Taken aback that any male would notice something like that, Nicki couldn't think of anything to say other than. "Ummm."

Unfortunately, Maxie didn't have the same problem.

"It's a blouse, not a shirt, dear," she corrected. "And you *have* seen Nicki in it, because she owns one. And well before Suzanne showed up in hers."

"It's a very popular pattern." Nicki didn't want to get into another argument about Suzanne's choice of clothing. "And most blouses pretty much look the same."

"That depends on who's wearing them," Matt said. "And I think Alex might be right. That woman back there is crazy, and she should be near the top of the suspect list."

"I'll be sure to let Alex know you agree with her."

"After her behavior today, I'm not so sure I don't agree with Alex and Matt as well," Maxie said. "I was mortified when she threw herself at Matt that way. Why, he's a good ten years her junior, and she should have been much more discreet."

"Discreet?" Nicki's eyes lit with amusement. "You mean like waiting until she'd cornered him alone?"

"Yeah. Like that was going to happen." Matt cast a mournful eye into the now-empty paper bag he'd grabbed out of Nicki's hands. "Where to now, Sherlock? And I hope it has something to do with lunch."

"It does." Nicki nodded before smiling at Maxie. "Could we head to the square? You could make good on your promise to buy Matt lunch."

"And what will you be doing while we're eating?" The question came from the direction of the back seat.

"Nothing that will require bodyguard duty," Nicki assured him. "I need to talk to the chief and let him know what we've discovered so far."

"If you're hoping he'll reciprocate and share what he knows with you, I wouldn't get my hopes up. Chief Turnlow doesn't strike me as the information-sharing sort." Matt laughed. "Especially when you come without your usual bribe."

Nicki reached down and lifted up a second paper bag for him to see, carefully holding it over the dashboard and out of his reach. "Oh. I wouldn't say that."

"Hey! You were holding out on me." Matt made a swipe for the bag, but Nicki had already dropped it back to the floor.

Maxie laughed as she pulled into one of the "official business" parking spots in front of the small police station. "We'll be over at the deli when you're through. And be sure to tell Danny that you're here to talk to the chief, so he'd better not write up a parking ticket."

Nicki gave a small salute as she hurried up the walkway, carrying her bag of treats.

Fran looked up from the stack of papers on her desk and smiled when Nicki walked in the door. "What can I do for you, Nicki?"

"I'd like to talk to the chief, if he has a few minutes to spare."

A voice bellowed down the short hallway. "If that's Nicki Connors, send her on back here, Fran."

The desk clerk winked at Nicki. "I guess he has a few minutes. That man hates to do paperwork, and any excuse to get out of it suits him just fine. So you take whatever you have in that bag right on back and see if you can put him in a better mood."

"Thanks. And Maxie wants Danny to know he can't write her a parking ticket."

"I'll let him know." Fran chuckled as she shooed Nicki away.

Nicki found the chief sitting in his usual place, surrounded by a mountain of paper.

She eyed the tall stacks, thinking it was against the whole idea of gravity that a couple of the lopsided mounds didn't tumble right over. "I had no idea there was this much crime in Soldoff."

"There isn't. But there's a lot of it in the State capital. Having to fill out this much paperwork for our annual funding should be a crime. And I'd sure enjoy arresting the guy who sits around all day dreaming up ways to make my life miserable."

Nicki set the paper bag down on one of the few clear spots on his desk. "Maybe these will help."

The chief smiled. "What did you bring, and what's it going to cost me?"

"Brownies and nothing," Nicki said. "Unless you want to share something with me, of course."

He reached into the bag and pulled out a large chocolate

square. "Looks great." He put it down and leaned back in his chair. "What is it you want to know?"

Nicki folded her hands in her lap and looked steadily back at him. "If you're going to arrest Charlie for Catherine's murder."

The chief sighed and ran a large hand through his thinning hair. "You know I can't tell you anything about that. And I don't want to lie to you, so find something else to ask."

Nicki sighed. What she had to tell the chief wasn't going to help poor Charlie's case at all. "Matt spoke with Beatrice Riley, the woman who lives in the house across the street from Catherine's?"

"I know Miss Riley. She has a reputation of being the town busybody."

She was sure the chief had gotten that very description from myMason. The retired chief and the current one kept in close touch. "She told Matt that she didn't see anyone except Catherine go in or out of her house that night. Not even after Rob and I found the body."

"So you think it was a ghost?"

Nicki gave him an exasperated look. "No. I think someone could have slipped in and out while she was fixing her dinner around five, or watching the news at six. But whoever it was, was gone by the time Rob and I came along."

"Then you're saying you didn't scare off a burglar?"

"I'm pretty sure we didn't."

"And since nothing else was taken, robbery wasn't the motive. Generally, that would leave greed, jealousy or revenge for some slight." The chief leaned forward. "Got someone in mind, Sherlock?"

He means someone besides Charlie, the boyfriend, Nicki thought. "Not yet. But I know that neither Ramona nor Cynthia Dunton have alibis for the night Catherine was murdered. And Ramona was mad at her mother for refusing to give her the money to study abroad for a year. Now she doesn't have that problem."

Nicki was grateful when the chief sat up a bit straighter. "Oh? Why is that?"

"Because control over the trust now passes to Cynthia, and she's already agreed to give her niece the money."

"Is that right?" The chief's eyes narrowed as he reached into the bag for a brownie. He took a large bite and chewed in silence for a full minute. "I think that might call for another chat with Miss Ramona Dunton."

CHAPTER SEVENTEEN

NICKI WALKED INTO THE ONLY DELICATESSEN IN TOWN AND looked around for Maxie and Matt. She spotted them sitting at a table against the far wall, right under a giant plastic fish. She waved, then walked up to the counter and purchased a bottle of sparkling water before joining them, taking the chair that was the furthest away from the tail of the fish that jutted out from the wall. Matt eyed her water as she twisted off the cap before raising his gaze to hers.

"Not much nutrition in a bottle of water."

"A lot of calories in that pastrami sandwich," Nicki retorted.

Matt looked down at his plate and then over toward the counter where a bored teenager was ringing up orders. "I can get you a turkey sandwich. Put something solid in your stomach and not as many calories." He grinned at her. "I'll even have them leave off the mayo, although that might be a crime against nature when eating a deli sandwich."

She smiled and her mood lightened up a bit at his determination to feed her. But she really wasn't hungry, and she had a rule not to eat unless she was. A rule she and Alex both adhered to, while ignoring Jenna's ability to eat anything at any time and still never gain an ounce. "Thanks, but I'm not hungry. Unlike you, I had breakfast."

"I had half an English muffin and half a cup of coffee. Can you honestly tell me you had much more than that?"

"I can." Nicki paused and waited until Matt had taken a large bite of his sandwich. "I had a full cup of coffee."

She grinned while he chewed furiously and glared at her, pointing at the ordering counter while she continued to shake her head.

Maxie clapped her hands together. "Now children, let's play nicely together. Stop teasing him, Nicki. He's an engineer who only grew up with brothers, so he has no idea that's what you're doing." She shifted her attention to Matt. "And Nicki isn't one of those New York models who starve themselves by eating a handful of lettuce once a day. She simply isn't hungry, dear. So enjoy your lunch, and let her drink her water in peace."

Having settled that matter, Maxie pushed her unfinished sandwich toward Matt. "Here. You can finish mine as well while Nicki tells us what the chief had to say."

Nicki sighed. She knew what the chief had to say, or more importantly what he had refused to say, would not make Maxie happy. "He didn't come right out and admit it, but I'm sure he's taking a good look at Charlie as a prime suspect"

"Why that's simply ridiculous. I might go in and talk to Paul Turnlow myself. Or maybe I should have my Mason give him a call."

Nicki perked up at that thought. The former police chief weighing in on Charlie's side was sure to count a lot in his favor. "That's a great idea! I know the chief really respects your husband's opinion."

"As he should. What else did he say?"

"That he was going to pay Ramona another visit to ask about the trust her father left her." Nicki shrugged. "I might have dropped a hint or two about it."

"Why hint around? Why didn't you just come out and tell him

that when her mother was alive, Ramona couldn't get her hands on the funds to go to Europe, and now that her mother's dead, she can?" Matt dropped his crushed napkin onto his empty plate. "Did you tell him what Beatrice said?"

"I told him. He didn't seem surprised that it probably didn't involve a robbery. But then he seems to have his attention fixed on Charlie." Nicki sagged back down again. She really didn't think that nice older man had killed Catherine in a jealous rage, or over an argument that had gotten way out of hand. "I wish I could talk to Ramona again."

"I must admit that I don't know why, dear." Maxie frowned at her. "I didn't find the young woman very pleasant to talk to. And she certainly didn't seem very upset over losing her only parent."

"I think she's more upset than she's willing to show." Nicki thought back over the small signs of Ramona's inner turmoil. "She kept looking away, as if she was trying to keep us from seeing the tears in her eyes. And when she picked up a coffee cup, her hand was shaking. I don't think she's staying with her aunt because she was bored at her friend's place. I think she doesn't want to stay in the house where her mother was killed, and she doesn't have anywhere else to go."

"This is an area where you have some experience," Matt said quietly. "If you think she needs help, I can find out the name of a good therapist in the area. Or maybe Alex could recommend one."

Nicki smiled her thanks at him. "That's a good idea. I also think she might know something about her mom's murder, and not even realize it."

"So Sherlock wants to ask her the right questions? Your side-kick thinks that's a great idea. If I remember the murder board correctly, we only have the ex-husband left to track down. And since he has an art gallery here in town, that shouldn't be too hard to do."

"And Suzanne told me she'd already spoken to Walter about you coming to see him before I had a chance to. But I might have an idea how to get into Cynthia's house to talk to Ramona,"

Maxie volunteered. "I'll set that up, but it does come with a price, dear."

"So what kind of bribe will I be baking now?" Nicki laughed.

"Raspberry tarts," Matt threw out, then ducked his head when both women stared at him.

"Raspberry tarts? It really isn't the right season for those, Matt." Nicki narrowed her eyes at the suddenly guilty look on his face. "Are you telling me you weren't kidding, and you *did* offer them to Beatrice Riley? Have you been promising bribes without any authorization, Dr. Watson?"

"I might have." Matt held his hands up in surrender. "All right. I did. I told you Beatrice had heard Nicki used treats to get information. She almost demanded to know why I didn't bring any with me. What could I do?"

Nicki put her hands on her hips and blew out an exasperated breath. "Offer something that's in season?"

Now Matt gave her an exasperated look of his own. "Sorry. She just threw it out there, so I didn't have a chance to download the raspberry-growing season chart off the internet."

"I'll have my Mason track some down. Just put them on your list. And don't forget to make a note of how much you'll need."

Nicki frowned in confusion. "What list?"

"The one you'll need to make for all the ingredients you'll need. But don't worry, dear. I told Addie she'll need to send someone by first thing in the morning to pick up the list and do the shopping."

"Maxie." Nicki reached out and covered one of her landlady's hands with her own. "Why do I need a shopping list, and why is Addie doing the shopping?"

"Or someone she delegates that chore to." Maxie blinked at Nicki's exasperated stare. "Remember that price I mentioned? Well. While I'm arranging a meeting with Ramona, you'll need to do a little baking. Just eight or nine items should do the trick. Suzanne did manage to put together a few other commitments."

Nicki fell back against her chair. "Eight or nine? Is this for our charity event? Because it's on Saturday."

"I know, dear. But when Addie called in a near panic this morning, what could I do but come up with a solution?" Maxie flipped her hands over so she could hold onto Nicki's. "I know the schedule will be tight, but I'm sure we can all manage. Addie will have the shopping done tomorrow by noon. I was firm on that. Then you'll have a whole day and a half to get the baking done."

"Saturday is three days away, Maxie, not a day and a half." Nicki was doing some calculating in her head. It *was* for a charity event, so she wanted to help all she could, but she would need another pair of hands. And right now was not a good time to ask Jenna to pitch in. She turned and gave Matt the once-over.

"What?"

"Does the job of sidekick include being my baking assistant?"

"Um." Matt scratched his head.

Nicki could almost hear the wheels turning frantically in his mind as he searched for an excuse. She looked away and pretended not to notice when Maxie kicked him under the table.

He grimaced slightly before forcing out a smile. "Sure it does. I'd be happy to help out with the Society's Literacy for Kids cause." He gave her a wink. "After all, you're creating future readers for the magazine."

Nicki smiled before nodding to Maxie. "Okay. My sidekick and I will give it a good try."

"Do or do not. There is no 'try'." Maxie laughed. "It's one of my favorite movie lines." She rose and gathered up her purse and sweater. "I will see you later this evening when I come by to help update the murder board and pick up your list. In the meantime, I'll see about arranging for us to pay Ramona a visit tomorrow afternoon. If you drop in on the ex-husband in the morning, then I'm sure we'll have all the information we'll need to catch Catherine's killer." She bent and brushed a kiss across Nicki's cheek and then did the same to Matt. "Try not to argue too much, children." She smiled at them both before heading out the door.

Nicki turned to Matt with her mouth formed into an "O".

"Did Maxie just say she expected us to solve this murder by Friday?"

Matt stared right back at her. "I think so. Did she just quote Yoda from Star Wars?"

CHAPTER EIGHTEEN

Nicki was mixing batter in a bowl and nibbling half-heartedly on carrots and hummus when the front door of her townhouse slammed shut. She chuckled and went right on scraping the sides of the bowl as the sound of Jenna's flip-flops tracked her approach to the kitchen.

"Hey!" Jenna lifted her nose and sniffed the air. "Are you making my favorite peanut butter bars?"

"Maxie drafted me into baking a whole store of desserts for the charity event. I had several bags of peanuts I bought for the cooking demonstration, so I thought I'd put them to use now and just have Addie replace them tomorrow." She slapped Jenna's hand away when she tried to peek under the dishcloth covering a bowl sitting next to the blender.

"Is that homemade peanut butter?"

"You know that's the only way to make the bars properly." Nicki scooped up the bowl and popped it into the refrigerator.

"So what's in that bowl?" Jenna pointed to the one in the mixer stand.

"Batter for a sheet cake."

"And what's in that little cup beside those carrots? Are you making carrot cake?"

Nicki laughed. "It's hummus, and it's my dinner."

"Not anymore it isn't." Jenna plopped a bag from Eddie's Burger Diner onto the counter. "You can have a sparkling water to satisfy your inner 'must-be-healthy' voice, but right now, what you need is good red meat and a little company."

"Did Maxie call and tell you she'd roped me into baking half the night?" Nicki , debated with herself about trading her hummus for grease and calories on a bun. But it was a very delicious grease and calorie concoction, and she was in the mood for something more satisfying than hummus and carrots. Giving in, she reached into an upper cabinet and took down two plates.

"That's the spirit." Jenna beamed at her. "And no, Maxie didn't call me. Matt did."

"Matt?" Nicki gave her friend a puzzled look. "What did he say?"

"That you were upset about the chief making Charlie his prime suspect, and that I should come over and take your mind off this whole murder thing for a few hours. Those were his words. He also said I should be sure you ate something besides a handful of lettuce for dinner. When did he become your food monitor, anyway?"

Nicki shook her head. "I have no idea. You should have heard him trying to convince me to eat a deli sandwich for lunch. You'd think I was wasting away to skin and bones the way he was talking."

"Well then, I won't tell him how I got you to eat a hamburger. It might hurt his feelings. Especially if he hears about the fries." Jenna upended the bag and dumped a mountain of French fries onto the kitchen counter.

Giving up all pretense of eating anything healthy for the evening, Nicki walked over to the refrigerator and got out a bottle of ketchup. She dug in right along with Jenna, and enjoyed every bite. Apparently grease and calories were exactly what she'd needed.

"I know Matt said not to talk about the murder, but what he doesn't know won't hurt him." Jenna put her burger down and used a napkin Nicki had supplied, to wipe a dribble of grease off her chin. "Besides Charlie, and of course finding the body, what else is bothering you about all of this?"

"Everything. Nothing makes sense. I mean, would a daughter really kill her mother just to get money to go abroad for a year? Why wouldn't she just whine long enough until Catherine caved in? That first day Alex and I talked to Suzanne, she said that's what Ramona had always done in the past, and her mother had always caved. So why kill her this time around? But Ramona doesn't have an alibi for that night. Neither does Catherine's twin sister, and neither does Charlie." Nicki got off her high stool and started to pace around the kitchen. "At least we can eliminate Mario. He *did* have an alibi. He was at the restaurant all night."

"And he doesn't really have much of a motive," Jenna pointed out. "Catherine bought into an investment that wasn't going to grow much. It seemed like an impulse thing on her part."

Nicki nodded her agreement. "I thought so, too. When she talked about it at the Society luncheon, it almost seemed like entertainment to her. I think she would have sold it back to Mario sooner rather than later. He even said so when I asked him about it."

"And I don't get the knife at all." Nicki resumed her pacing. "I'm sure it wasn't Catherine's. There wasn't another one even close to that one in quality in her knife drawer. And every one I saw in there was dull. Alex said the knife used to kill Catherine was not only very high quality and expensive, it was also extremely sharp. But why would the killer bring it?"

"Um... to stab his intended victim?"

"But that would mean the murder was premeditated. Why wouldn't the killer bring a hunting knife? It's made to kill things. Why an expensive chef's knife? And why was Catherine acting so strange at the restaurant? Even the waiter said she seemed completely distracted. Why?"

"I don't know," Jenna said. "But Matt was right. This whole thing is going to drive you crazy. After we've finished our burgers, let's go have some fun. I left my laptop next to the hallway table. I say we set it up and try out a couple of these programs Trident sells. Jeff gave me a copy of most of their software. Except for the stuff still under development." She wiggled her eyebrows at Nicki. "Wouldn't you like to see what Rob or Matt will look like in thirty years? It might influence which one you'll let stick around."

"Funny. But sure, I'd like to see this stuff you've been raving about for the last week. Why don't you get your laptop while I put this sheet cake into the oven?" As Jenna disappeared into the hall-way, Nicki called after her, "and get ready to explain when he went from 'the giant client' to 'Jeff.'"

———

AN HOUR LATER NICKI WAS LAUGHING SO HARD THAT TEARS were rolling down her face. Jenna had turned Matt's future likeness into a silver-haired supermodel, while Rob had come out looking like a cross between Homer Simpson and Mr. Magoo.

"That's just mean, Jenna," Nicki declared once she could draw a complete breath. "Rob would never let himself go like that, and Matt looks like he stepped out of a Hollywood movie. And without his glasses."

"Not a problem." Jenna tapped a few keys and Matt's glasses suddenly appeared on the face of the silver-haired stud staring back from the screen. The computer geek tilted her head and studied the image. "I think he looks better with the glasses. Maybe he shouldn't undergo that fantastic new procedure that my future world has developed to make everyone's eyesight perfect."

"Along with their hair, nose, eyes and everything else." Nicki grinned. "Except for poor Rob."

"Lover-boy has the soul of a troll, so he deserves to look

like one."

"That's very poetic and once again, not nice." Nicki leaned forward and tapped the key to bring up the other images they'd already played with. "But this age enhancement program really is amazing."

Jenna had scanned in one of Nicki's pictures when she was five-years-old, and the computer had produced an image of what she would look like today. Except for a slight difference in the hair color, it was almost perfect. In fact, it was so close, Nicki's jaw had almost dropped all the way to the floor. Jenna showed her the same age progression she'd done on one of her own childhood photos, with the same result.

"The facial recognition program is even better. It analyzes different points on your face then matches those to thousands of pictures. I'd show it to you, but we don't happen to have a database with thousands of pictures in it."

Nicki sat back and took a sip of her wine. This whole "get away from the murder thing" had helped her relax for the first time since she'd found Catherine slumped over her pasta dinner. She hadn't realized how wound up she'd become, and made a mental note to thank Matt not only for the idea, but for calling Jenna about it.

"What else can these programs do beside project a face into the future?" Nicki was genuinely interested in what Jenna was going to showcase in the new website she was designing for the mysterious Jeff at Trident Industries.

"It has a wardrobe and style program." Jenna tapped some keys and up popped another set of icons to choose from. "Go stand over by that wall so I can take your picture, and I'll show you what this can do."

Nicki did as she was told and stood patiently while Jenna snapped a photo of her standing and then another close-up of her head and shoulders. While her friend was uploading the images to her computer, Nicki poured them both another glass of wine and pulled the second sheet cake out of the oven. Leaving it on the counter to cool, she set the timer for thirty minutes before rejoining Jenna on the sofa in the living room.

"Okay. All set." Jenna brought up the image of Nicki standing next to the wall. "So here's the high-tech way to select your wardrobe for the day." Jenna started changing Nicki's outfit, sticking with pants and blouses, since that was what she'd been wearing when the picture was taken. Nicki laughed when her image suddenly appeared in a full-length ball gown, with a skirt that sparkled to go along with the tiara Jenna had put in her hair.

"Now you know what you'd look like as a princess." Jenna grinned at her friend. "Not a bad look for you."

"But it would look better on you. That dress would be so much more striking with your height and darker coloring. I look like a washed-out cake-topper."

Jenna snorted. "You'd never look like a washed-out anything. You've got a show-stopping face, and figure that would look great in a wheat sack."

"Hmm. I might have to try that sometime, just to prove you wrong. What else have you got?"

"Let's try the style enhancement program." Jenna pulled up Nicki's head and shoulders picture, and turned her from a honey-blond into a darker brunette. Then she gave her long curly locks and put a streak of blue in her hair, starting from her forehead and curling down past her shoulder. "Now you can see what you'd look like if you ran with a punk crowd instead of your staid and steady friends."

Nicki scooted closer to the screen and studied the image for a long moment. "Can you pull a picture off the internet and do this same thing?"

"Certainly. Do you have someone in mind?"

Nicki nodded. "Do a Google search on Cynthia Dunton from San Francisco."

"Uh oh. Sounds like we're back to murder."

"Just curious." Nicki watched as Jenna switched to the search engine and began looking for an image of Cynthia. They were in luck when they came across an old staff photo for the public library in the city.

"This should work," Jenna said under her breath as she pulled the photo into the application built by Trident. "Okay. What would you like to do?"

Nicki pursed her lips and closed her eyes, pulling up an image of Catherine in her mind, before looking back at the librarian's picture on the computer. "Make her hair lighter. Can you put in highlights and then make the eyebrows narrower?"

They worked on the picture for several minutes until Jenna sat back and softly whistled. "Wow. I wouldn't be able to tell her apart from Catherine."

"Well, they are twins, so that's not so surprising," Nicki said. "I just hadn't realized how much they look alike."

"Me neither. At least not from that photo."

Nicki continued to study the image until she shook her head. "A picture doesn't always tell the whole story." At Jenna's questioning look, she shrugged. "Right now you wouldn't even recognize Cynthia, if all you had to go on was that photo. She's got pitch-black hair that's cut into a short and shaggy kind of style."

Jenna glanced back at the image on the screen and frowned. "Why? That would look terrible with her coloring."

"Some kind of hair disaster, although I can't imagine that it looked worse than it is now. But Ramona liked the Goth look on her aunt and Catherine did not, from what Cynthia said. But there's more to it than just a hairstyle. They have different taste in clothes and makeup, and Cynthia walks with a slight stoop in her shoulders while Catherine didn't. It was a lot of little things that made them so different from each other."

"Okay, I get that." Jenna sniffed the air. "If it's about time to frost those cakes, I call dibs on the bowl."

Nicki laughed. "What are you, Jenna Lindstrom? Five years old?"

Jenna closed the laptop and stood up. "If it gets me the frosting bowl, being five years old works for me."

CHAPTER NINETEEN

"I GUESS THIS IS THE DAY WE TALK TO THE EX-HUSBAND. THE guy who owns the art gallery, right?" Matt glanced at the large silver watch on his wrist. "It's still early. He might not have opened up yet."

Nicki glanced across the square. She and Matt were standing outside his hotel, enjoying a patch of morning sunshine as they planned out their day. She'd met him in the hotel lobby, leaving her townhouse right after she'd pulled the peanut butter bars out of the oven and left them cooling on the counter.

She smiled when he stifled a huge yawn. Despite all the hours he was putting in trailing her and her friends around town, Nicki was sure Matt still worked late into the night on magazine business. The thought gave her a case of the guilts, which she appeased by pointing at the Starbucks on the other side of the square. "We can get a cup of coffee while I fill you in on our baking schedule for tomorrow, and what Maxie said about making a quick run out to see Ramona this afternoon."

"Sounds good. A walk and talk, followed by a cup of coffee, works."

He strolled alongside her, automatically shortening his steps so

Nicki didn't have to run to keep up with him. "How much baking do we need to get done?"

Nicki laughed. He sounded as if he was about to take a march to the gallows. "Not as much as you're obviously dreading. I made two sheet cakes last night, and finished off the peanut butter bars this morning. So that leaves the raspberry tarts, which I fully intend to leave to you, with detailed instructions and close over-sight of course, and only three more items on our to-do list. Since we don't have to go shopping for any of the ingredients, it shouldn't take us too long. And I may tackle one of them tonight, while you're slaving away on magazine business." She stopped just short of the doorway into Starbucks. "It shouldn't take us more than a few hours on Friday morning, so you'll have most of the day free to work on your agenda for the festival in L.A. I'll even throw in pizza and beer for you to take back to the hotel if it will help. And you won't get that offer once Alex gets here for the weekend."

"Alex's arrival means nothing but health food?" Matt sighed.

"Health food and healthy lifestyle. That means running in the morning and tofu for lunch."

When Matt looked horrified, Nicki burst into laughter. "I'm kidding. Alex can eat a whole batch of zucchini fries in one sitting."

"Zucchini and fries are two words that shouldn't be in the same sentence," Matt declared, holding the door into Starbucks open for her.

Nicki gave him a quick pat on the cheek as she passed by him. "You might really like them."

"Uh huh."

They'd ordered their coffee and were back on the sidewalk, cardboard cups in hand, within a few minutes. Matt took a short sip and then frowned down at his cup.

"Is something wrong with your coffee?" Nicki asked.

"How come yours tastes so much better?" He frowned at her. "I have a sneaking suspicion I'm not going to like normal coffee anymore."

"My coffee is perfectly normal."

Matt didn't bother to answer but looked around the square instead. "So where's this art gallery located?"

"Down that little side street over there." Nicki pointed to their left. "He usually comes in early, so he should be there by now."

"Then you've been to this gallery before?" Matt asked as they slowly walked toward the next corner. "What kind of art does he feature?"

"Mostly his own, although occasionally he'll display another artist's work."

"Great. Then I won't mention that I've never heard of the artist when he points out one of his own paintings."

"Here we are." Nicki stopped in front of a whole wall made up of one big window, with large red letters shadowed in black, spelling out "The Walter Gifford Gallery" across the entire front. Two potted palms in heavily glazed ceramic pots, stood on either side of the entrance, along with a short length of red carpet that made an eye-catching splash of color against the drab sidewalk.

Matt rolled his eyes when he spotted the carpet. "A nutcase for a best friend, the worst winemaker in America for a boyfriend, and now some guy full of himself for an ex-husband. Catherine wasn't much good at judging character."

"Suzanne's just upset and lonely without her best friend. Charlie may not make good wine, but he does grow beautiful roses, along with being a very nice man, and all artists have huge egos. You should know that since you've interviewed enough of them."

Matt smiled at her. "You're right. No judgements here." He opened the door to the gallery and ushered her inside.

Walter Gifford sat behind a small writing desk located in the center of the room. He looked up when the bell over the door tinkled. A thick fall of deep brown hair was tucked behind his ears and hung down to his shoulders. A prominent brow and forehead gave him the look of an artist, which he played up even more by wearing a black cape with red satin lining over his t-shirt and jeans.

"Nicki, isn't it?" His deep voice boomed out across the floor.

"You have an entertaining little blog on the local establishments, and write for that magazine on the internet."

He stood up and waited for Nicki and Matt to cross over to him.

Nicki politely held out her hand only to have it enveloped in his much larger one. He smoothly flipped it over and placed a lingering kiss on the inside of her wrist. Not comfortable with the intimate gesture, Nicki quickly snatched her hand back. Beside her, Matt went perfectly still.

"This is Matt Dillon," Nicki quickly made the introduction.

"Her close friend." Matt put an emphasis on the word "close". Nicki had no intention of correcting Matt's hint that he was more than just a friend. Not if it would encourage Walter to keep his hands, and his lips, to himself.

"He's also the editor and owner of that magazine on the internet." Nicki kept her voice and her stare cool as she looked around. The wall was adorned with abstract paintings, all done in bold colors. Despite his poor manners and oversized opinion of himself, there was a reason a Gifford painting sold very well. They really were striking. "You have some lovely paintings. Are they all yours?"

"Naturally. I had another artist's work in here last week, but it was overwhelmed by my paintings, so I had to take them down." Walter sat at his desk and pointed to the two chairs in front of it. "Have a seat. I doubt if you're here to discuss art."

"Is there something else you think we should be discussing?" Once Nicki sat, he took up a position behind her chair, standing with his arms crossed and his gaze fixed on the artist.

Ignoring him, Walter addressed Nicki. "Suzanne called a few days ago. She told me you were looking into Catherine's murder and I should expect a visit. Since Chief Turnlow's already been here, I've just been waiting for your arrival."

"Oh good. Then we can get right to our questions and not take up any more of your time than necessary."

"Or ours," Matt said, not bothering to keep his voice low.

Nicki cleared her throat. "Yes. We do have a full schedule

today. Maybe we could start by asking where you were on the night Catherine was murdered?"

"Right here, conducting a private showing for three potential buyers. They'd admired my work in Dallas, and happened to be in town on a wine tasting tour. I've already given their names to the chief if you'd like to check with him on whether or not my alibi holds up."

Nicki mentally marked *alibi* off her list and moved on. "I understand there were bad feelings between you and Catherine?"

Walter gave her an amused look. "Hence the reason we got a divorce."

"I meant specifically over some investment losses," Nicki clarified, raising one eyebrow when his lips and jaw tightened. It looked like she'd hit a nerve. "Suzanne talks to us too."

"And about private matters, it seems," Walter groused. "One of her more annoying habits. And yes, I was understandably put out when the investment money I entrusted to Catherine dropped significantly in value."

"How significantly?" Matt asked.

Walter gave him a hard look. "About one hundred thousand dollars' worth, not that it's any of your business."

"People have been killed for less than that," Matt said.

"Not by me," Walter shot back before deliberately returning his attention to Nicki. "Is that all your questions?"

Nicki turned around and shook her head at the man standing behind her. "Behave, Matt." All she got in response was a grunt.

Looking amused, Walter leaned back in his chair with a smirk on his lips. "I didn't try to hide my feelings on the matter. Catherine knew how I felt about her negligence in handling my money."

"Your money? Weren't the two of you married?"

The flamboyant artist laughed. "That's a very charming and very outdated concept, Nicki. Being married doesn't mean you have to share your assets. Since I was her second husband, and she was my third wife, we chose not to." He glared up at Matt. "And before you start putting out the theory I had my ex-wife killed as revenge for costing me so much money, Catherine and I had already come to an agreement about that, and it's all written down and legally filed as part of the divorce settlement. I didn't fight her on retaining a number of my paintings she'd acquired by various means through the years, and she had it put in her will that their ownership would revert back to me. Their worth should cover the monetary loss I suffered at her hands."

"Which you couldn't rectify until she died. Which she did. Very convenient."

"Matt!" Nicki's sharp tone rang through the gallery. "I asked you to behave." She turned back to Walter and smiled. "I'm sorry. Just one more thing." When the artist raised a questioning eyebrow, she went on. "What do you know about the trust set up by Ramona's father?"

He shrugged. "There isn't much to know. It was set up under Catherine's oversight to distribute as she saw fit. I believe her daughter will come into the bulk of it when she turns thirty."

Nicki nodded. That's exactly what Maxie had said. "What about now? Since Catherine can no longer administer the trust?"

Walter frowned and ran a hand down the side of his face. "I have no idea. I suppose the timetable would be stepped up and Ramona would get the money now. Or maybe someone else will be appointed to oversee it until her thirtieth birthday."

"So you've never seen Catherine's will?"

"I've seen it. A copy is part of the divorce settlement. But I've only read the parts that pertain to me. I really am not interested in what Ramona does, or doesn't, inherit."

"Then you didn't know that Cynthia is the new administrator for the trust? She said she had a copy of the will and it specified that."

Walter chuckled and shifted his cape so it hung down the sides of his chair. "If Catherine gave Cynthia a copy of her will, that would be shocking. The two of them shared very little, at least not while Catherine and I were married. Except of course going to those auctions together." Walter made a point of looking at his watch.

"I saw a receipt from an auction house on Catherine's desk," Nicki said quickly. "It listed the purchase as a doll."

Walter nodded. "Catherine collected them, if the price was right. I suppose Cynthia did too, although she must have spent a great deal more than my former wife did because a couple of times a year she'd ask Catherine for more of her share of the money under old man Dunton's trust." He gave a distinct sniff. "I guess a librarian's pension for collectible items doesn't stretch too far."

"Cynthia asked Catherine for money?" That took Nicki by surprise. She thought Suzanne has been exaggerating when she'd mentioned that. Especially after meeting Cynthia. Nicki would've bet that Catherine's twin lived very modestly, and probably by choice. So why would she need more money in addition to her pension and what was most likely a regular allowance from her father's trust?

"Whenever she asked, Catherine always gave it to her, as far as I know. Probably because she didn't ask as nearly as often as Ramona did. That girl must have sent her mother a request every month for more money to buy something or other, or to travel somewhere. She's a definite money pit. Once she does get her hands on the bulk of her trust, I don't expect it to last very long." This time he didn't just glance at his watch but held it up for Nicki to see. "I really need to wrap this up. I have another appointment."

Nicki rose and walked around the chair, taking Matt's hand in hers. "Thank you for your time, Walter."

At the other man's curt, bordering-on-rude nod, Matt's mouth turned down into a scowl. Seeing it, Nicki quickly tugged on his hand and pulled him toward the door. Without even a backwards glance, she got her annoyed editor out onto the sidewalk in front of the gallery. She dropped his hand and turned to face him, her own hands now on her hips.

"What is the matter with you? You can't be my sidekick if you alienate our suspects."

Matt's scowl turned up at the corners. "Hey! I sat in Beatrice's rickety chair, put up with Suzanne almost plastering herself all over me, drank Charlie's foul-tasting wine, and just now I didn't deck Walter I'm-a-pig Gifford. I'd say I'm a great sidekick."

Nicki rolled her eyes and started walking back toward the hotel.

Matt fell into step beside her. "Am I detecting a sudden interest in Cynthia on your part?"

"I don't know. She doesn't have an alibi, and maybe even has a motive if you count her own trust, but from what Walter said, it doesn't sound like it. But then there was the Trident program."

"What's the Trident program?"

Nicki proceeded to explain the astonishing results from matching Catherine's hair and make-up onto Cynthia's face, finishing up by repeating a good part of the discussion she'd had with Jenna about it.

Matt was silent for a moment, and Nicki was content to stay the same way while he thought it all through.

"Well," he finally said. "I guess the similarity is to be expected since they are, or I mean they were, twins. But then like you said, looks aren't everything."

Nicki smiled up at him, sure he was completely unaware that he'd voiced a sentiment near and dear to her own heart.

"No. They aren't."

CHAPTER TWENTY

"I HOPE YOU DON'T MIND THAT MATT ISN'T COMING ALONG with us to call on Ramona," Maxie said from the passenger seat of Nicki's small Toyota.

"Of course not," Nicki assured her. "Despite his firm belief we need a guy with us at all times, he doesn't need to tag along every place we go."

Maxie's mouth turned down at the corners. "He's such a nice boy. I thought you liked him."

Nicki took her eyes off the road just long enough to frown at her landlady. "I do like him. A lot. You know that."

The older woman smiled. "Of course I do, dear. I just wanted to make sure that you knew it too. He's quite taken with you, if you don't mind the use of an old-fashioned term. 'Taken' falls somewhere between like and love, although he's leaning well toward the love side."

"Maxie!" Nicki closed her eyes and prayed for patience. Really. Talking about Matt and love in the same breath was crossing way too far over the line. "If you say anything like that to him, he'll probably keel over from a heart attack. You're reading too much into our friendship, because that's all it is."

"And you're still reading too little into it, dear." Maxie shook her head. "But no matter. You'll come around. That's our turn, right past those large trees."

Nicki maneuvered her little car around the corner, onto a quiet residential street with small houses on large lots.

"Cynthia lives in the third house down on your left. Yes. I believe that's Ramona's car in the driveway. She told me it isn't in working order at the moment."

Nicki pulled in beside the black Honda. She waited the usual five seconds after she'd turned the engine off for it to stop sputtering and completely shut down. Telling herself for the hundredth time that she really was going to need to replace her car sometime next year for sure, Nicki pushed open the door while Maxie did the same on the opposite side. After their short, separate wrestling matches with the doors, they both managed to get out of the vehicle and step onto the driveway. Nicki paused to take a look at the house and yard. The lot was spacious and sparsely landscaped, with only a single small tree growing between the house and the road. The house itself was very much in the same box-like, cookie-cutter plan used in mass-produced, subdivision housing.

Nicki hurried over to take the carton filled with programs that Maxie had hauled out of the back seat. On the front of each one was a picture of Catherine, wearing a jaunty pillbox hat and smiling into the camera. Maxie put a gentle hand on Nicki's shoulder.

"Ramona picked out that picture and selected some very appropriate and tasteful music for the service. I think you were right about her hiding her real feelings over her mother's passing."

"I know how she feels. There were days after mom died that I just wanted to ignore the whole thing." Nicki's smile was thin and sad. "I thought if I didn't acknowledge it, then it never happened. I think Ramona is going through the same gamut of emotions, and she really thinks she can outrun the pain by going to Europe."

She stopped at the front door and waited for Maxie to ring the bell. It wasn't long before Ramona swung the door open, her green-striped hair pulled back into a ponytail making her look closer to a teenager than a twenty-six-year-old. Her red-rimmed eyes told Nicki that she'd been crying.

Ramona stepped back and jerked a thumb toward the interior of the house. "Come in. Aunt Cynthia isn't here, and I'm not sure when she's coming back. I think she went to see about her hair again." Nicki and Maxie followed her down a short hallway that opened up into a compact living room. There was a TV sitting on top of a stand that looked as if it first landed in that spot sometime in the 1950s. It was flanked on either side by two display cases, while the opposite wall had a sofa and La-Z-Boy recliner. Aside from a couple of tables and lamps, that was all there was to the room.

Ramona hunched her shoulders slightly and followed Nicki's gaze. "My aunt doesn't like to throw anything away, or buy new things if the old ones are still working."

Nicki set the box down and wandered over to the display case nearest the opening that led into the dining room. The case had probably been an open bookshelf at some point, but now it held five Madame Alexander dolls. Nicki recognized a couple of them as the same ones on display at Catherine's house. She glanced over at the second case. It was tall with glass doors and held several shelves of books. *Not surprising since Cynthia was a librarian*, Nicki thought. She walked back to the recliner and took a seat on its edge as Maxie reached for one of the programs from the box Nicki had set on the table.

"I hope you like this, dear. I think it came out very well. And everyone loved the picture and the music you picked out."

"They did?"

Ramona sounded so surprised that Nicki had to smile. She guessed the young woman wasn't used to much praise from her mother's friends. Nicki had a suspicion that Suzanne didn't think much of Ramona and probably let it show.

"I'm sure your mother would be very happy with what you helped arrange," Nicki said gently.

Ramona shrugged. "I think I should have done more, but Suzanne was so...." She paused and shook her head.

"Pushy? Opinionated? Forward?" Maxie supplied, making Ramona laugh.

"Yes, she was." Ramona wore the first genuine-looking smile Nicki had seen on her. Thinking that was progress, Nicki gave her a warm smile in return.

"It's been hard," the young woman confessed in a small voice. "Suzanne's been kind of over the top. She acts like she's lost her soul mate, while Aunt Cynthia doesn't seem to care much at all, and mom was *her* twin." Ramona shook her head, making her ponytail bounce across the tops of her shoulders. "But all my aunt seems to care about is her collection."

Nicki glanced over at the dolls. "I saw some of the same ones in your mom's house, so I guess that was something they had in common."

"I think she just bought those dolls to bug mom." Ramona waved a hand toward the other side of the TV. "It's her book collection she talks about all the time. But then what would you expect from a librarian? Books are all she's ever talked about."

Nicki could hardly take issue with that, since she'd had the very same thought herself only a few moments ago.

"Yes, librarians do seem as obsessed with books as I am with family letters and photos when I'm doing my genealogy research." Maxie gave Nicki a long look. "Would you mind bringing a glass of cold water to me, and maybe one for Ramona as well. I can see the kitchen right though that doorway." She turned her smile on Ramona. "Where does your aunt keep her glasses?"

"In the cupboard next to the sink, but there isn't an icemaker in the fridge door. You'll have to open the refrigerator up and scoop the ice out of its bucket."

"No problem." Nicki gave one last, speculative look to the bookcase before walking toward the kitchen.

While Maxie kept up a stream of conversation with Ramona, Nicki quickly searched through all the kitchen drawers, and even took a quick look into the small pantry, but she didn't find one knife to match the same brand as the one that was used to kill Catherine. Even the set displayed in the butcher block on the counter was a far inferior quality than the Zelite knife found at the crime scene.

Having hit another dead end in her theories, Nicki quickly filled two glasses with ice and then water, before hurrying back to the living room.

"I like it, Mrs. Edwards. I think mom would too." Ramona looked up when Nicki handed her a glass of water. "Thanks." She held it up to her lips and watched Nicki over its rim. "The chief said that your mom was murdered too."

"Yes, she was. And I have no idea where my dad is, so he wasn't much help. But I have two of the best friends in the world, and they helped me through it. They still do."

"Oh." Ramona fell silent, looking down into her drinking glass. "I have a friend like that. I've known her since grade school. I was staying with her when... well... when..." Ramona stumbled to a stop and took a deep breath. "You know, that night. I'd still be hanging at her place except Aunt Cynthia insisted that I stay with her."

Nicki picked up her purse and fished around for the folded piece of paper she'd slipped inside it earlier that day. Setting her purse down again, she handed the paper to Ramona.

"My friend Alex is a doctor. She recommended a grief counselor who happens to be right here in Sonoma. This is his name, number and address, if you'd like to talk to someone."

Ramona's fingers curled around the paper and without a word she tucked it inside her jeans pocket.

"The other number on there is my cell phone. Call me anytime you want to talk," Nicki added.

Ramona stared at her and smiled just a little. "Maybe. Thanks. Suzanne said you were doing some investigating into the murder."

"A little. Mostly to help Chief Turnlow."

"My aunt said you've found a dead person before."

Nicki nodded, but she wasn't too thrilled with the turn of the conversation. She didn't think it would do Ramona any good to talk about dead bodies, so she glanced over at Maxie. "If you have everything you need, we should get going. I know you still have a lot of work to do for the event on Saturday."

"Yes. And you have baking to get to." Maxie took Ramona's hands into her own. "The Ladies in Writing Society is hosting a charity event this weekend. Lots of demonstrations and things to buy. If you feel up to it, I hope you'll join us. Nicki is giving cooking demonstrations all day Saturday, and has made a lot of the treats that will be on sale. Since this was an event your mother was a co-chairman on, it would be perfectly appropriate for you to make an appearance in her honor."

Ramona took a deep breath and bit her lower lip. Nicki thought she looked close to tears again.

"Maybe I will. Aunt Cynthia likes to cook. Maybe she'd come with me."

Maxie gave her hands one last squeeze before busily gathering up the rest of the programs and tucking them away into the box. "That would be just fine then."

Nicki rose as well and picked the box up off the table. "Thank you for letting us come over today. I know it isn't easy seeing people after you lose someone you love."

Ramona nodded but didn't move from her spot on the sofa. Maxie gave her a motherly pat on the shoulder.

"We'll see ourselves out, dear. Don't forget about Saturday."

They made their way out of the house and back to the car. They'd barely settled in when Ramona came flying down the walkway.

"Wait, wait!" She waved her arms as she sprinted for the car.

Nicki rolled down the window just as Ramona skidded to a stop next to her.

Catherine's daughter leaned over and put a piece of paper onto the dashboard. "That's my cell number. If you find out anything about who killed my mom, would you call me?"

"Of course I will," Nicki said without a moment's hesitation.

"That's good. Thanks." Putting her hands in her pockets, Ramona stepped back. She gave them a nod as Nicki backed her car out of the driveway.

They were almost halfway home before Maxie ventured a comment. "That was a nice thing you did, dear, giving her the name and number of a grief counselor."

"She'll need one if she's sitting in that house crying alone. And it was Matt's idea. He's the one who called Alex and gave me the information before I came to pick you up."

Maxie settled more comfortably into her seat. "He's such a nice boy, isn't he? And a thoughtful one too."

"Yes, Maxie. He is." Nicki rolled her eyes. She really wished everyone would stop campaigning on Matt's behalf and let him do it himself. If he was so inclined. Which Nicki didn't think that he was.

"Well, back to business then. Did you find anything in the kitchen?"

Nicki shook her head. "Some knives, but nothing out of the ordinary. And none of them were nearly as pricey as a Zelite."

"I'm not surprised, dear. What about Walter? The ex-husband is always a good suspect."

Walter had come off as being just short of slimy, but he didn't impress Nicki as a killer. "He can recoup his financial losses, but only if Catherine is dead."

"Really? Why, that's an excellent motive!" Maxie sounded almost cheerful over the prospect.

"But," Nicki added, "he has an ironclad alibi he's already given to the chief, who I'm sure thoroughly checked it out."

Maxie slumped back against her seat. "Oh. How unfortunate, since that still leaves Charlie as the main suspect." She sighed and stared out at the landscape passing by the window. "What do we do now?"

Nicki wished she knew.

CHAPTER TWENTY-ONE

"WOULD YOU LIKE AN APRON?" NICKI HAD TO SMILE AT THE look of resignation on Matt's face.

He put his hands in his pockets and hunched his shoulders in. "I suppose it has ruffles all around the border?"

"You haven't just stepped into an episode of *The Brady Bunch*, Matt. I have chef aprons, and they don't come with ruffles or lace."

Matt grinned at her. "Might not be so bad. Marsha was pretty hot."

"Marsha, Marsha, Marsha," Nicki chanted. She handed an apron to Matt before donning one herself and adjusting the ties around her slim waist.

Matt followed her example before he rested his hands on top of the long quartz counter. "I don't know why you'd take issue with Marsha. If you'd been on the show, that would definitely be the role you'd be cast in."

Nicki cocked her head to one side and considered it for a moment. "Maybe. But I'd rather be Alice."

That put the grin back on his face. "The one with the hairnet and sensible shoes?"

"And the only one who ever got anything done on that show. At least she put a meal on the table." Nicki pulled out a stacked set of mixing bowls from a cabinet in the base of the island. "Including dessert. Which we are about to make. And when it comes to raspberry tarts, by 'we', I mean you."

She produced an index card and set it on a small stand on the counter. "Here's your recipe. All you have to do is follow it. But check with me before you do anything." Nicki gave her tall, dark-haired kitchen assistant a stern look. "And I mean anything."

Matt picked up the card and read through it before looking up and smiling. "This doesn't look so hard."

Already seeing a problem looming ahead, Nicki narrowed her eyes and put her hands on her hips. "Did I mention to check with me before you do anything?"

"Yes, boss. You did." Matt returned the card to the little stand and leaned against the counter.

"What kind of cooking do you do when you're at home?"

"The peel-back-the-cover-and-stick-it-in-the-microwave kind. My list of numbers for takeout is very long." Matt's grin was back in place. "But don't let that scare you. I'm a fast learner."

"But a slow starter," Nicki said before she realized she'd said it out loud. She quickly got busy taking out several sets of measuring spoons and plugging in the mixer and blender.

Matt adjusted his glasses and shuffled his feet. "Um. We are still talking about cooking, aren't we?"

Nicki took a quick breath before glancing over at him. "Yes. And you can start by getting together everything you'll need and putting it all in one spot. The dry ingredients are on the table, and the raspberries and butter are in the fridge."

"Where did you find the raspberries?" Matt asked as he claimed a set of the measuring spoons and one of the bowls.

"Not that one, it's too small. Try this one." Nicki handed him a bigger bowl. "I didn't find them. Addie did, at the grocery store. But she almost fainted at the price."

Matt frowned. "If they busted the budget, I'll be happy to pay for them. Consider it my contribution toward the cause."

She smiled. It was so typical of Matt to offer to buy all the raspberries. "No need. We'll just up the price a little and sell every delicious tart. Provided of course..."

"I know," Matt said, cutting her off. "Provided I check with you before I do anything."

Nicki beamed at him. "That's the spirit!"

The morning flew by as they worked companionably side-by-side. Matt grumbled, but he checked with Nicki before he measured even a teaspoon of salt. He teased her about her complete lack of sports knowledge, and she returned the favor by giving him a thorough description of the plot of her favorite Sherlock Holmes adventure.

Just as Matt had carefully, and holding his breath the entire time, set his first batch of tarts onto a cooling rack, the front door slammed shut. He gave his new creations a nervous look before lifting his gaze to Nicki's smiling face.

"That was loud. Are these going to, I don't know, fall down inside or something?"

"They're tarts, oh great sports czar, not soufflés." She kept right on stirring her caramel sauce when Jenna burst through the door.

"I could smell all this deliciousness even through the walls." She walked over, sat down and snatched a tart right off the cooling rack before Matt could stop her.

"Hey! We're going to sell these."

Jenna shrugged and put her stolen goodie on the counter, waving her hand back and forth to help it cool. "Put it on my account."

"You don't have an account." Matt carefully pushed the rack holding his tarts out of Jenna's long reach.

"Then I guess you'll have to chalk it up to a business loss and cover it yourself."

"Sounds like a good plan," Nicki said. She kept stirring even as she bent over to give her sauce a closer look. "I think this is ready." She nodded to Matt. "Go ahead and put in the next sheet of your tarts and set the timer to forty minutes." She switched her attention to Jenna. "Are you on a break from your website design marathon?"

"I'm ahead of schedule, actually, so I needed a break."

"How would you like to earn that tartlet?" Nicki turned her head slightly so she could keep an eye on Matt as he slid the next batch of tarts into the oven. She wanted to be sure he set the timer. Matt was meticulous when it came to details, which made him a good editor and, she supposed, a good engineer as well. But he was out of his element in the kitchen. Besides, she enjoyed bossing him around.

And it was beyond adorable the way he took each task so seriously. She'd watched him out of the corner of her eye when he'd measured out the sugar three times, and then had squatted down to get eye level with it, just to be sure he got it right. Even now he was standing, wiping his hands continuously on a dish towel as he held his breath when Jenna took her first bite of his creation.

"Wow! Seriously scrumptious." Jenna gave him a thumbs-up as she took a second bite, and Matt's whole face lit up with a huge smile.

"I had some help," he admitted, aiming his smile at Nicki.

"Don't tell anyone that," Jenna said around a mouthful of tart. "It will ruin your rep."

Matt immediately held his hands up. "I don't want a rep. This is a onetime only experience."

"Uh huh." Jenna finished off her tart and wiped her hands on a paper towel. "So what do I have to do to show my appreciation for Matt's one and only creation?"

Nicki inclined her head toward the hallway as she continued to drizzle caramel over the last few cupcakes in front of her. "Help us update the murder board. I can tell you from personal experience that Matt's handwriting is almost as bad as Alex's."

Jenna's head whipped around and she pointed at him. "Then you are not to go near the board. Ever."

She hopped off her stool and headed for the door. Nicki quickly untied her apron and followed, with Matt right behind her.

Once Jenna had the marker in her hand, she faced her audience of two. "What's new? What do we add and where do we add it?"

"Walter Gifford. He has a big motive for wanting his ex-wife dead since he's named in the will. He not only gets his paintings back, but he believes they'll cover the one hundred thousand dollars he lost from bad investments Catherine had made." Nicki paused while Jenna wrote it all down.

When she was finished, Jenna stepped back and nodded. "That's a dandy motive. Better than anyone else's. So the crime is solved?"

"He has a solid alibi," Matt put in. "He was with potential art buyers at the time."

"Then the crime isn't solved." Jenna stepped back up to the board. "Is there anything else we know?"

Nicki consulted the little notebook she always carried with her and used to jot down the highlights of any event or interview. "Cynthia and Ramona are both beneficiaries of separate trusts that Catherine had control of, and both used to ask her for additional funds, although Cynthia only occasionally and Ramona on a regular basis."

Jenna waved for her to continue as she kept writing out notations on the board.

"Gifford's a creep." Matt shrugged when Nicki shook her head at him.

"No judgments, remember?" she said, although she had to agree with him. Catherine's ex-husband was not someone she'd want to meet in a dark alley.

"That's not a judgment, that's a fact."

Jenna chuckled as she wrote "creep" next to Walter Gifford's name. "I guess the interview didn't go all that smoothly."

"Because my sidekick didn't behave very well," Nicki sighed.

"Your sidekick didn't like the way he put his hands on you, or talked down to you."

"Oh really?" Jenna turned around and frowned at Nicki. "Then as your friend, I have to agree with the sidekick." She looked over at Matt. "As Nicki's friend, I'm wondering why you didn't smash in Walter's artistic nose?"

Matt shrugged. "Nicki said 'no'."

"And back to our murder," Nicki said loudly. "Like her twin, Cynthia also collects dolls, and according to Ramona, she collects books, too, and likes to cook. But, she didn't have any high-end knives in her kitchen."

"Bummer. No knives and no motive unless you think she wanted to get control of the trust?"

Nicki shook her head as she put her notebook aside. "She doesn't have to. According to Walter, Catherine gave her the extra money whenever she asked."

Jenna walked over to the small sofa and plopped down next to Matt. "So where's the connection? What do we know for sure?"

Nicki stared at the board, her mind working to find those elusive "dots" that would tie everything together. "It isn't what we know, it's what we don't know."

"Such as?" Matt asked.

Nicki stood and walked over to the board. Her eyebrows drew together, and she pressed her lips into a thin line as she read several of the entries before facing Jenna and Matt.

"We don't know why Catherine was acting so out of sorts the night she was killed, or who she was supposed to have met with that day, despite the fact she tells her best friend, Suzanne, everything. And we don't know where the knife came from that was used to kill a woman who doesn't cook. And we don't know how a killer not only got into the house, but out again, without being seen by Beatrice Riley. And we don't know why Catherine was killed, except it wasn't a robbery."

"We do know she was stabbed in the back," Matt said quietly. "That might have been convenience, or it might be for a reason."

"Revenge?" Nicki turned back toward the board. "But by who? And for what?"

"Money." Matt nodded when Nicki sent him a questioning look. "There's six suspects up there. A daughter, a sister, an ex-husband, a business partner, a boyfriend and a best friend. And four out of six of them had a money issue with Catherine Dunton. So that gives it a better than fifty-fifty chance it was for money."

"I vote for the ex," Jenna declared "He has enough bank to have hired someone to do the deed. And once a creep, always a creep."

"I'm leaning toward Ramona," Matt said.

Startled, Nicki frowned. "Why? Have you even met her?"

"Kids do stupid things when they're mad at their parents. Look at the Menendez brothers, or Lizzie Borden for that matter. Ramona would have known about the nosy neighbor and her daily schedule, and if anyone knows how to sneak into a house without being seen, it's a kid."

Although very logical, Nicki still shook her head. "I've talked with her, Matt. She didn't kill her mother."

"Who do *you* think did?" Jenna asked.

"If Alex were here, she'd vote for Suzanne. So that would be three different opinions and three different conclusions." She crossed the room and sat back down in her desk chair. "I don't know who did it. I only know I'm sure it wasn't Ramona Dunton or Charlie Freeman."

They were all staring at the board when Nicki's cell phone rang. She glanced at the caller ID before she tapped on the answer button.

"Hi, Maxie."

"Nicki, this is Mason Edwards. I'm using Maxie's phone. She asked me to call you."

Clutching her phone tighter and pressing it more firmly to her ear, Nicki jumped up from her chair. "Is she all right?"

"She's upset, but she's fine." Mason paused for a moment and Nicki tensed when she heard him suck in a breath.

"Maxie wanted me to let you know that I got a call from Chief Turnlow a few minutes ago. He's arrested Charlie for Catherine's murder."

CHAPTER TWENTY-TWO

AFTER MASON HAD HUNG UP, NICKI HELD HER PHONE OUT AND stared at it.

Both Matt and Jenna jumped to their feet and rushed across the room.

Jenna put her arms around her friend's shoulders and pulled her close in a protective gesture. "What's wrong? What's happened? Is Maxie okay?"

"She's fine. Maxie is fine." Nicki's voice was flat. "It's Charlie." She looked up at Matt who was standing in front of her. "Chief Turnlow has arrested poor Charlie."

"The boyfriend? That nice old guy with the really bad wine?" Jenna exclaimed. "Why him?"

"I don't know." Nicki could feel the bubble of anger growing.

This has to be killing Maxie, she thought. And the bubble rose higher. Clenching her fists, the anger mixed with helplessness. Charlie. That loveable old bachelor who'd never hurt any living thing in his life. Maxie's friend, who Nicki had promised to keep clear of the investigation. Within a minute Nicki was so angry and frustrated, she couldn't keep a fat tear from rolling down her cheek.

"Oh shit," Matt said under his breath just as the oven timer went off in the kitchen.

When he didn't move, Jenna darted a look between his face and Nicki's before pushing her friend forward until her forehead bumped against Matt's chest. "Find out what's going on while I get the tarts out of the oven."

Looking like he was on the edge of panic, Matt opened his mouth and shut it again before he simply put his arms around Nicki, drawing her close.

Nicki was so grateful for the comfort, that she circled her arms around his waist. He quietly rested one cheek on top of her head and just let her cry her anger and frustration out, even if he did wince at every tear soaking into his shirt. It didn't take long for the sudden storm of emotion to blow through, and Nicki stood quietly, her arms still around Matt and his around her, as she gathered up her scattered thoughts.

When she sniffled loudly and then sighed, he leaned back far enough to be able to look into her face. "Feel better?"

"Yes. Thank you." She knew she sounded pathetic, but right now she really didn't care, and didn't make any protest when he led her over to the sofa and urged her to sit. Once he'd managed that, he strode over to the desk and grabbed the chair along with a box of tissues he spotted next to the computer.

Pushing the chair over to the sofa, he sat down directly in front of her and set the tissue box on the cushion right next to her. He waited silently while she dabbed at her face, and when her hand dropped back down into her lap, still clutching a tissue, he put one hand on her knee and with the other used two fingers to lift her chin so she'd meet his worried gaze.

"What's going on?"

"I'm just angry, Matt. I promised Maxie we'd help Charlie stay out of jail. And now that's exactly where he is. I let her down. I let them both down." Nicki sniffed again and raised the tissue to dab some more at her eyes, blinking rapidly to hold back a fresh surge of tears. "I hate letting people down."

"I do know that about you, but I don't think Maxie is going to blame you because Charlie got arrested. She's more likely to blame Chief Turnlow."

"I promised her, Matt. And you've met Charlie. He didn't do this. I know he didn't do this, but I don't know what I can do to help him." Nicki turned her head to the side and closed her eyes. "I can't imagine that sweet old man being dragged off and withering away all alone in a jail cell."

When Nicki turned her gaze back to him, Matt's lips were clamped tightly together. He looked as if he was trying not to burst out laughing. Nicki's eyes narrowed. Okay. Maybe that had been a bit dramatic, but if he laughed, she swore she'd kick him in the shin and never give him another double fudge brownie for as long as he lived.

Fortunately for Matt's future chocolate intake, he managed to get the impulse under control.

"Honey, we don't know if Charlie did or didn't kill his girlfriend. All we know for sure is that he's been arrested. We don't even know why he was arrested. Last time you talked with the chief, all he could say about Charlie was that he was Catherine's boyfriend, who's approaching seventy, with no solid alibi, and maybe left a few fingerprints around her place. Hardly seems like enough to arrest a guy. Especially for a cop with as much homicide experience as the chief has."

Nicki blinked and then stared at him, her eyes wide. Her tears dried up and the color rushed back into her face. When she tried to stand, he got to his feet, shoving the office chair backwards with one quick kick as he pulled her up with him. She knew she caught him by surprise when she rose on her toes and planted a soft kiss square on his lips. She drew back and smiled when he just stood there, staring down into her upturned face.

"Thank you, Matt. You're right. We don't know what the chief has on Charlie and standing here crying isn't going to help him. It's just that Maxie is special. She's... well, she's..."

"Like a second mother?" He smiled. "Yeah. To me too."

When she skirted around him, he quickly turned and frowned as she went to her desk and picked up her cell phone.

"And I suppose you intend to do something to help him? If it involves getting into a car, then I'm doing the driving. I don't want you spending any more time than necessary in that rundown excuse of a car that you own." He ran a hand through his hair, leaving strands sticking up in its wake. "I'm going to have nightmares about you being stranded on a dark road somewhere because of that car."

He looked more resigned than surprised when she answered him with a "to see the chief." But he did shake his head at the next thing out of her mouth.

"Jenna needs to get back to work and you need to get ready to fly to L.A. tomorrow. I'll be fine going into town in broad daylight."

"Correction." Matt crossed his arms over his chest. "*We* will be going into town in broad daylight, and *I* will decide whether or not I'm going to L.A. tomorrow."

"Second correction," Jenna said from the doorway. "*Jenna* will decide if she needs to get back to work or not, and *I* am deciding 'not'. So I'm going with you. And Alex and Ty will be on their way here in a couple of hours." Jenna held up her cell phone. "I just talked to her."

"We can call Maxie on our way into town and let her know what we're up to," Matt said. "We'd better get going."

———

"GLOVE? WHAT GLOVE?" NICKI LEANED OVER THE CHIEF'S DESK, sparks flying out of her eyes. Between her office and arriving at the police station, Nicki had gone from frustrated tears to fuming and back again.

She didn't care what evidence the chief had. Charlie Freeman did not kill anyone. She knew it, and she was positive the chief knew it too. He'd been a homicide detective for over twenty years, how could he not know Charlie wasn't a murderer?

The chief sighed and gestured for her to sit back down. When she didn't comply, he looked over at Matt.

The next thing she knew she'd been pulled back into the chair next to her editor, and he was leaning down close enough she could feel his breath on her cheek.

"Calm down, Sherlock. We need information, and we aren't going to get it if you antagonize the chief."

"She might," the chief huffed out. "I've been sitting here expecting you for the last hour. Ever since I called Mason. I'm surprised it took you so long to get here."

"We had to get over the shock first," Jenna said. She had the same glare as Nicki fixed on the chief. "All this brouhaha over a glove?"

Chief Turnlow folded his hands on top of his desk and looked calmly back at the tall computer whiz with the big glasses. "A glove with Catherine Dunton's blood on it, found on a bench in Charlie's greenhouse. And his prints found in Mrs. Dunton's dining room."

"Anyone could have planted that glove, Chief," Nicki said. Only Matt's heavy hand on top of her leg was keeping her in her seat. "And he was Catherine's boyfriend. Of course you'd find his fingerprints in a lot of the rooms in her house."

"We only dusted the dining room and the door handles, Nicki, so those are the ones that count, and Charlie's prints showed up. He can't prove where he was that night, and we *did* find that glove. I can't ignore all that." The chief leaned back and ran a hand through his hair. Thanks to Matt, because he did the same thing, it was a habit Nicki had come to recognize as a sure sign that the chief was frustrated.

"It doesn't matter what I think. Those are the facts."

Nicki settled down a little and studied him for a moment. "What do *you* think, Chief? Off the record." She smiled when he rolled his eyes, but he looked to Matt for his agreement to keep everything "off the record", and then to Jenna, who held up three fingers."

"Scouts honor that mum's the word."

"I suppose that's the same scout troop that Nicki was in?" the chief said in a dry tone before running his hand over the top of his head again. "I don't think Charlie is guilty. I'd be surprised if he ever swatted a fly, much less killed another human being."

"Then why did you arrest him?" Jenna demanded.

"Glove, fingerprints, possibly a jealous motive."

"Jealous?" *Charlie?* Nicki thought the chief was way, way out in left field on that one.

"Suzanne Abbott stated for the record that a lot of other men were attracted to Catherine, and her friend was constantly fending them off whenever they went out on a girl's night. Even though she was married. It could be argued that maybe Mrs. Dunton didn't turn all of them down."

"Then maybe you should look at the ex-husband who gives slime ball a new meaning," Matt said.

"Have to agree with you there. But we didn't find that glove in his gallery."

Nicki snorted. "Charlie wasn't jealous of anybody, and someone planted that glove to make him look guilty. All we have to do is figure out who."

"I hope you can, Nicki. And I'm going to keep poking around, too. In the meantime, Charlie stays under arrest, and it will be up to the county prosecutor whether or not the evidence is enough to keep him in jail."

THE RIDE BACK TO NICKI'S TOWNHOUSE WAS A QUIET ONE. BOTH she and Jenna spent most of the fifteen minutes staring out the window. As they turned into the drive leading onto the Edwards' property, Nicki couldn't help but sigh.

"What am I going to tell Maxie? Charlie's in jail and I don't have any idea who killed Catherine."

"Neither does the chief of police," Matt pointed out. "And he has a lot more resources at his disposal."

"Well, whatever we're going to say to Maxie we'd better come up with it quick. That's her car in front of the townhouse," Jenna said.

Nicki's head snapped around to the forward windshield as Matt approached the cul-de-sac that housed half of the townhouses in Maxie's writer's colony, including the two that Nicki and Jenna occupied. Sure enough, the landlady's late-model Mercedes was behind her little Toyota in the driveway, and partially sticking out into the street. Since neither Maxie nor her husband were anywhere in sight, Nicki thought they were probably waiting for them inside.

While she didn't drag her feet up the walkway, she wasn't exactly making good time either. Until Matt came up behind her, grabbed her arm, and propelled her along.

"Come on, Nicki. She's not going to yell at you."

"You mean the way you did when you were upset with me over George Lancer's murder investigation?" Nicki snapped her mouth shut. It really wasn't fair of her to bring that up, but she wasn't in the mood to take it back, so she settled on just being quiet.

"Yeah." Matt kept her moving along. "But I apologized."

At the front door Nicki dug her heels in and faced him. "And I should too. I'm sorry. I shouldn't take my nerves out on you."

"We'll just put that one in the bank against a future misstep on my part."

Nicki smiled her agreement as he opened the door. She got just a foot inside before she was enveloped in a giant hug. Recognizing Maxie's perfume, which was all she could manage since her face was buried in the silk covering Maxie's shoulder, Nicki relaxed under a wave of relief and hugged her landlady right back.

Maxie finally stepped away and held Nicki at arm's length. "I can't tell you how wonderful it is that you went down to the police station and gave Chief Turnlow a good piece of your mind for arresting Charlie. It's exactly what I wanted to do, but was prevented by an immovable force." She looked over Nicki's head and glared at her husband.

Mason Edwards only smiled at his wife as he shook Matt's hand. "It's good to see you again, son."

"You too, sir." Matt grinned. "I'm glad it's not me who's in the doghouse this time."

"I won't be for long. I'm just waiting for a callback from Bart Rivers."

"Who's Bart Rivers?" Jenna asked as she came up behind Matt.

Mason smiled and nodded his head in greeting. "Hello, Jenna. Bart's our lawyer. His office is in San Francisco, and he's arranging for a good defense attorney for Charlie. After that's all fixed up, Charlie should be out on bail within a few hours."

"But in the meantime, our good friend is sitting in the hoosegow, with who knows what sort of lowlifes and serial killers," Maxie declared, waving her arms for emphasis.

"Hoosegow?" Jenna repeated.

"It's an old western term for jail," Mason explained. "And Chief Parks in Santa Rosa assured me Charlie is quite comfortable in his own cell, by himself, and far away from all those 'lowlifes and serial killers'. Paul made it a special request when he took Charlie over there himself." He shook his head. "Last time Chief Parks looked in on him, Charlie was playing cards with one of the guards who was on his lunch break."

Nicki smiled at that. She could imagine Charlie thinking of this whole thing as a unique adventure. But being accused of murder was no joke, and unless a better candidate came along, Charlie might spend the rest of his retirement years behind bars.

"MyMason's arranging for an attorney to get bail set, but I can tell by the tone in his voice that it isn't looking good for Charlie," Maxie said before shifting her gaze to Nicki. "Do we have any idea who might have done this?"

Nicki bit her lip as she gave a quick shake of her head. "Not a one. Before your husband called, we'd just gone over everything we *don't* know. It's a much longer list than what we know for sure."

The older woman sighed long and deep. "That's not going to let me sleep well tonight." She glanced toward the kitchen. "I think it's time to break out your chocolate stash."

"And chips," Jenna chimed in. "We can make a full confession to Alex when she gets here."

Just then Nicki's phone rang, with the distinct ring tone of Carol King's *You're So Far Away*. Before hitting the answer button, she swiftly pointed toward the kitchen. "Go ahead and get started, Jenna knows where the stash is." Nicki walked into her office as the others filed toward the back and the kitchen.

It was less than five minutes later that Nicki joined them. She plucked a chocolate-covered peanut from the pile in front of Jenna and thought about making a big pot of coffee. As she rounded the corner of the island she frowned.

"Where's Matt?"

Maxie lifted her gaze to the ceiling while her husband looked at his feet. Only Jenna didn't seem to be bothered by her question.

Her longtime friend separated her pile of candy and shoved half of it over toward Nicki. "He left. He said he had a plane to catch, and to tell you that he'd see you later." Jenna popped a chocolate in her mouth and raised an eyebrow at her friend. "I'm guessing that Matt knows the ring tone you use for lover-boy."

CHAPTER TWENTY-THREE

NICKI LOOKED AROUND THE LARGE BARN. IT HAD BEEN TURNED into the local exhibition and event hall a number of years ago by the town council. It kept a modest income rolling in to the city and gave the various groups in the area a place to hold their events, rather than renting out space at one of the nearby wineries.

It was late in the afternoon, and she was about to start her second cooking demonstration for the day. She'd hoped that Matt would make it back to Soldoff in time to see it, but so far he hadn't made an appearance. Jenna and Maxie both had told her he didn't look happy went he'd left so abruptly.

As the day marched toward evening, and she hadn't seen or heard from him, she'd begun to wonder if maybe he'd decided to stay in L.A. for the rest of the food and wine festival afterall, and then return to Kansas City from there. She was almost tempted to call his very scary assistant, Jane, and ask her if Matt had changed his travel plans. Almost.

Jenna had helped her with the first demonstration set-up, and Nicki had been pleased, and a bit humbled, at the large number of people who'd been willing to sit through it. She hoped to have the same success the second time around. Now it was Alex who was digging through her bin, having volunteered to be Nicki's go-fer and gal Friday for the second demo while Jenna and Ty were exploring the rest of the exhibits, and of course the bake sale and food court.

Alex was stacking several bowls and a platter on the large counter where Nicki would be making her shrimp scampi, along with a couple of side dishes she'd decided would go over well with the crowd.

"Did I tell you I spent yesterday at the coroner's office? That's why Ty and I were able to get away sooner than expected." Alex looked down at the list Jenna had handed off to her and then started recounting the bowls.

Nicki looked up from where she was sorting through the large plastic bin supplied by Addie that was filled with the ingredients she'd need for all the dishes she would be demonstrating. "No, you didn't. How did that happen?"

"Dr. Tom was running very short-handed, so he called in the favor. The lead physician didn't mind since he had extra staff on for the day shift, so over to the ME's office I went."

Nicki shook her head. Even though she seemed to be stumbling across more than her share of them, she couldn't imagine spending a whole day with dead bodies. "Did it bring back memories of med school?"

Alex laughed. "An autopsy room is an autopsy room, and I saw the one at NYU enough when I was in training, including a stint in pathology during my year as an intern. But it was interesting getting a tour of the forensics lab, even if the one part was a little creepy."

Wondering just where Jenna had stashed the spice mix Nicki always blended herself, she looked around thinking maybe it had been left on the cooking table. "After working in an emergency room, what could be creepy about a lab?"

"There was a pair of black capri pants spread out on the work bench, and the tag had a case number and Catherine's name on it."

Spying the elusive jar at the far end of the table, Nicki walked over and grabbed it before she frowned at Alex. "What did you say?"

"Excuse me? You're Nicki Connors, aren't you? I recognized you from the other day."

A short woman with gray hair, an over-sized sweater, thick-soled shoes and a pink pastry box in her hands, stood next to the raised platform looking up at Nicki. Automatically smiling, Nicki nodded and took a step to the edge of the platform.

"Yes, I am. Can I help you?"

"I'm Beatrice Riley."

Nicki widened her smile. "It's nice to meet you Mrs. Riley, is there something..." Nicki paused and put one hand to her mouth. "Oh, Mrs. Riley. Catherine's neighbor from across the street?" Nicki sat down on the platform's edge and eased herself over the side until she was standing on the barn's floor. "I left your tarts over at the bake sale station."

Beatrice raised the pink box and nodded. "I got them without any fuss. Tried one, too. They're good enough that I thought I should come over and say 'thank you'." She nodded at Nicki. "Not everyone would've remembered a promise they made to an old lady, and a stranger at that. I wanted you to know I appreciate it. Any time you want to come over and chat, or need some more information, you just come knock on my door."

Nicki was charmed by the compliment, and thought Beatrice wasn't as bad as Maxie had painted her. "I should be fair and tell you that Matt made the raspberry tarts."

"With strict instructions from Nicki not to do a single thing until he checked with her," Alex called out. She grinned at Nicki. "Jenna told me."

Beatrice's whole face crinkled upward into a smile. "He's a nice boy. And you must be a good teacher. Wish I could stay to see this demonstration of yours, but I've got to get back to keep an eye on things."

"Of course," Nicki did her best to keep a serious look on her face. "I'm sure everyone in the neighborhood appreciates your diligence."

"So they should." Beatrice nodded and added another "thanks" before ambling off and disappearing into the crowd.

"I wish Matt had been here to say 'hello' to her." *But I'm glad Maxie was on the other side of the room*, Nicki thought, an amused smile on her lips.

"Well if you're looking for an entertaining conversation, here comes Jenna with Ty trailing after her." Alex looked around. "This platform is great for keeping track of everyone."

Jenna strolled up, a half-eaten muffin in her hand, while Tyler was just popping the last of his into his mouth. Alex shook her head at both of them.

"I suppose you're going to tell me that was the healthiest thing to eat that you could find."

Jenna turned and winked at the tall, solidly built man behind her. With his buzzcut and lopsided smile, Tyler Johnson looked every inch the fireman that he was.

"I don't have to answer that because she's not the boss of me," Jenna told him. "But *you* might have a problem."

"Ha, ha," Tyler said before he gestured for Alex to come closer. When his fiancée bent at the waist to hear what he wanted to tell her, he slipped a hand behind her neck and proceeded to give her a thorough kiss.

Jenna eyed them and shook her head. "Well, I guess that's one way of explaining things."

"Looks like a good way to me." Nicki laughed.

Jenna held up her muffin. "Speaking of good, you have some serious competition in the baking department. This orange-cranberry muffin rivals the one you make, and I didn't think I'd ever be able to say that." Jenna wrinkled her nose. "As a matter of fact, if I didn't know better, I would have sworn this *is* one of your muffins."

"Really?" Always interested in improving her own skills, Nicki playfully snatched it out of Jenna's hands.

"Hey, I was eating that," her friend complained, making a grab to get it back.

But Nicki had already danced away and was holding it out of her reach. "You can have the rest of it. I only want a bite to see why you think it's better than mine."

"I didn't say better, I said it was just as good." Jenna's eyes squinted behind her glasses when Nicki took a small bite and then frowned. "What's wrong? Can't figure out a secret ingredient?"

"Oh, I know these ingredients. I should." She split the rest of the muffin in half and studied the inside. "Uh huh. Whole and chopped cranberries, a taste of ginger, definitely fresh orange juice and turbinado sugar on top." Nicki pinned Jenna with a look. "Where did you get this?"

"I bought it over at the baking station."

Nicki glanced in that direction. "Who was selling them?"

"Suzanne Abbott." Jenna grabbed Nicki's arm before she could sprint off. "What's going on?"

Nicki shook her head and easily squirmed out of Jenna's hold. "I don't know yet. I'll tell you once I find out."

Nicki headed straight for the baking station. She quickly passed every table selling baked goods, but didn't see Suzanne anywhere. At the very last table she ran into Addie.

The pleasant, matronly woman beamed at Nicki. "It's going so well, and your demonstration was the hit of the event. So are your baked goods. I can't thank you enough for all your work, Nicki."

"It was no problem at all." Nicki kept looking around, trying to spot Suzanne in the sea of people. "Have you seen Suzanne?"

"Oh, you just missed her. She took some of the cashboxes over to the command booth for counting. You might catch her there."

"Thanks." Nicki did her best to thread her way through the crowd as fast as she could, heading for the tables set to form a square on the far side of the barn. She caught a glimpse of Suzanne coming out from behind one of them and heading for the large door that opened out onto the parking lot. Nicki picked up her pace even more, sending apologies out right and left as she plowed her way toward her quarry, finally catching up with her just before Suzanne stepped outside. Latching onto her arm, Nicki pulled the startled woman off to the side.

"Whatever's gotten into you, Nicki Connors? And let go of my arm, you're probably giving me a bruise."

Nicki stopped and stepped over until she was directly in front of the clearly flustered Suzanne. Holding the muffin up, Nicki kept her gaze fixed on the middle-aged woman's face. "Were you selling these? Jenna said you sold her this muffin."

"Yes. That's what I had in this plastic bin. But they're all gone now. Why? Was there something wrong with it?" Her lip stuck out in a pout. "Maybe they weren't as good as yours, but everyone raved about them, and I haven't had any complaints."

"Did you bake them?" Nicki asked, still closely watching Suzanne. Somehow, she just couldn't believe Suzanne had made the muffin she was holding in her hand.

Suzanne's lip stuck out even further. "What if I did? You aren't the only one who knows how to bake."

"Fine. Tell me what's in them?"

Catherine's best friend blinked, before she lifted her chin a notch. "Why should I?"

"Okay. Do you even know the name of the sugar on top of this muffin?"

Suzanne shrugged. "It's sugar. What else is there to know?"

"I know what kind of sugar it is, and I know what the special ingredient is that gives it that little kick." Nicki took a small step closer, forcing Suzanne to take one back. "Who made this muffin, Suzanne?"

"Oh all right. When I spoke with Cynthia a few days ago about the memorial service, I asked her if she'd like to contribute something in Catherine's name to the bake sale today. Catherine said more than once that her sister liked to cook. And Catherine *was* the co-chair for the event and all. Cynthia dropped a measly half-dozen of these off at my house this morning."

Nicki stepped back and her mouth dropped open. *Cynthia?*

Catherine's twin sister? Conversations began to play back in her head, and suddenly what hadn't made sense, started to make a lot of sense.

"Are we done? Or do I have to go through a grilling from all your friends, too?" Suzanne pointed behind Nicki, who turned and saw Jenna, Alex and Ty making their way through the crowd.

"Oh. We're done," Nicki told her. "Thanks for your help." Without another word to the pouting Suzanne, Nicki waved at her friends and then pointed to the open barn door. She headed outside, knowing they'd follow, and dug her cell phone out of her back pocket as she walked. Scrolling through her contacts, she found the one she wanted and tapped the dial button just as the other three came running up to her.

"What's going on?" Alex asked.

Nicki held up one hand as a voice came on the other end of the line.

"Hello? Ramona? This is Nicki Connors. Are you alone? Good. I need to ask you a couple of questions."

In less than two minutes Nicki was putting her phone back into her pocket. She turned to look at the three faces staring at her.

Jenna was the first to speak up with a clap of her hands. "You've figured it out, haven't you?"

Nicki slowly nodded. "I think Matt was right."

"Matt?" Ty frowned. "What did Matt say?"

"He said it was about the money, and that books are expensive."

"Books? Money? Nicki, what are you talking about?" Alex demanded. "What books? What money?"

Nicki focused on her doctor friend. "Didn't you say that you saw black capri pants in the forensic lab with Catherine's name on them?"

"Yes I did, along with a blue blouse," Alex confirmed. "Why? You would have seen the same ones since she was wearing them the night she died.

"I didn't really notice her pants when I was at her house," Nicki said. "But I did notice how nice she looked, which wasn't at all unusual for Catherine, when I saw her at the restaurant. Blue blouse, green pants."

"Green? Are you sure?" Jenna asked.

Nicki nodded. "I just called Ramona and confirmed that her mother owned a pair of green pants. Ramona bought them. They were a gift for Catherine's last birthday. But I'll bet they aren't in her closet now."

"So what does that mean? That she changed her clothes when she went home on her break?" Jenna shook her head. "Maybe she spilled something on them."

"Or maybe she wasn't wearing them," Nicki said. When Jenna looked like she was about to tear her hair out, Nicki smiled. "You were right too, Jenna. Those *were* my muffins. Or at least they were made from my muffin recipe. The very same one I gave to Catherine at the restaurant the night she died."

"Then how did Suzanne get it?" Jenna frowned.

"She never did get it, and she isn't the one who made those muffins. She just told me that Cynthia did." Nicki nodded when Jenna's jaw dropped open.

"Cynthia? Catherine's twin?" Alex reached for Ty's hand and held on.

"Holy shit." Her fiancé pulled Alex into his side and looked around as if he expected to see a knife-wielding Cynthia burst into view at any moment.

Nicki fished her car keys out of her pocket while she tossed out directions to her friends. "Jenna, can you please call the station and have them track down the chief and let him know about the muffin? And tell him I'm sure it was Cynthia at Antonio's that night, not Catherine, and he should search her house for the recipe card. It will have my chef's stamp on it." She looked over at Alex. "Can you find Maxie and let her know what's going on? Have her call Ramona and tell her to get out of that house and walk somewhere so the three of you can pick her up, while Jenna's locating

Chief Turnlow in all the festival madness in town." Nicki didn't like the idea at all of Ramona possibly being alone in the house with her aunt. She looked directly at Ty. "Please don't let anyone go into that house if Cynthia Dunton is there."

He nodded. "I won't."

"Wait, where are you going?" Alex demanded as Nicki turned away. "It's starting to get dark."

"Nothing dangerous. I'm just going to see if those pants are hanging in Catherine's closet, or if the chief should look for them over at Cynthia's place too. Remember, no confronting Cynthia! We'll leave that to the chief." Nicki gave a wave before heading for her car at a dead run.

"I thought Catherine's house was locked up and taped off as a crime scene. How's she going to get in?" Ty wondered out loud.

"Oh trust me," Jenna said, her phone to her ear. "She'll find a way."

CHAPTER TWENTY-FOUR

WHAT SHOULD HAVE BEEN A QUICK TEN-MINUTE RIDE, TOOK Nicki nearly double that as she skirted through back streets, trying to avoid the traffic snarl that went with festival days. When she finally reached Catherine's street, she still had to drive another two blocks before she found a space just large enough to squeeze her Toyota into. Trying not to draw too much attention to herself, she kept to a quick walk to cover the distance back to the place where she was certain one twin had murdered another. Half a block from her destination her cell phone rang. Glancing down at the caller ID, she debated with herself, but only for a second before she tapped the answer button and raised the phone to her ear.

"Matt. How's Los Angeles?"

"Don't play games with me, Nicki.

She blinked. She didn't need to see his face to know that Matt was clearly furious.

"Where are you? Because you aren't at the charity event, and all I got out of Jenna was 'she figured it out' before she spotted Chief Turnlow and took off."

Oh yeah. Make that *really* furious.

"I don't have time to explain or argue, Matt. I'm on my way to

Catherine's house. There isn't any reason for you to worry, I'm only going..."

"Fine," he snapped out. "I'm on my way. Don't you do anything that might get you into trouble until I get there."

When the phone went dead, she frowned. If he wanted to rush over here for nothing, he could do that. Then he'd see for himself she wasn't doing anything to get into trouble. All she was going to do was take a quick look through Catherine's closet. And maybe her laundry. Then she'd be on her way back to her own townhouse. Shaking her head at this new and annoying tendency in Matt to overreact to the strangest things, she continued down the block.

Just before she reached the Cape Cod style house, with crime scene tape crisscrossing the front door, Nicki crossed the street and skirted up a narrow walkway until she was standing in front of a door with faded green paint. Lifting one hand she gave a brisk knock, then stepped back and waited.

Ten minutes later she was standing on the front porch of Catherine's rental house, with the front door unlocked. She put one leg through a large gap in the tape and bending over until her nose almost touched her knee, she carefully slid her body through the opening. Thanking her lucky stars for having a petite frame, Nicki stood up and waved toward the big picture window in Beatrice Riley's house before closing the front door behind her. Thank heavens she'd remembered Matt telling her that Beatrice had a key to Catherine's house.

Bypassing the opening into the living room, she walked across the small entryway and straight up the stairs. She intended to be in and out before Matt made his appearance.

Lace curtains were draped across a window at the top of the stairs, and photographs of vineyards hung all along the hallway. Nicki turned to her left and followed the upper banister. She peeked into the first door, which looked like a guest bedroom, then continued past a bathroom with a pedestal tub, and on to the closed door at the end of the hallway. She opened it slowly and peeked around its edge. A queen-size bed took up most of the space, along with a mahogany bureau and two side tables. Since it was definitely the larger of the two bedrooms, Nicki guessed this one was Catherine's. There was only one other door in the bedroom and she went right over to it. On the other side she found exactly what she was looking for — Catherine's clothes closet.

She'd sorted through to the half-way point when she heard a loud creak directly behind her. Whirling around, Nicki's hand flew to her throat and her stomach did a sudden backflip with enough violence she had to brace a hand against the bedroom wall.

"I gather you're looking for something?" Cynthia Dunton stood in the doorway, her legs braced apart, and a very nasty-looking gun in her hand.

"I, I..." Nicki couldn't take her eyes off the gun. Straightening away from the wall, she automatically put her hands up.

"This isn't a hold-up, Nicki."

Cynthia actually sounded amused, which had Nicki's knees locking into place and her eyes narrowing. She didn't see one funny thing about pointing a gun at someone. Especially when it was pointed at her!

"Well?" Catherine's killer prompted. "What are you looking for?"

"Green pants. The ones you were wearing when you took Catherine's place as the hostess at Mario's."

Cynthia sighed and shook her head. "I should have thought of that. That you would notice the difference between what Catherine and I were wearing that night. I did my best to match her clothing, but she only had that one pair of black pants. But I thought a blue blouse and dark colored pants would work. It seems I underestimated your powers of observation. But then you weren't supposed to discover my dearly departed sister. Her boyfriend Charlie was, and since he never saw me at the restaurant, my slight difference in clothing shouldn't have made any difference."

"How did you know I was here?" Nicki was desperate to buy

some time, hoping Matt would hear them talking and realize what was going on, or maybe Beatrice had seen Cynthia come into the house and had already called for help.

"Suzanne called me." Cynthia gave a little wave of the gun. "She was very offended that you didn't believe she was capable of making those muffins. Why didn't you believe her, by the way?"

"You used my recipe."

Catherine's twin smiled. "A small conceit on my part. I just wanted to see if I could make a muffin people would rave about as much as they did for the ones made by the resident gourmet chef." She inclined her head toward Nicki. "And I did. But I only sent six of them to Suzanne. With you scheduled to put on all those cooking demonstrations, I didn't think there was any chance that you'd end up with one of them. A miscalculation on my part, I'm afraid."

"You made quite a few of them, Cynthia." When the older woman's gaze hardened, Nicki took a deep breath and did her best to act unconcerned about being held at gunpoint. She just needed to keep Cynthia's attention away from the man slowly moving up behind her. And of course come up with a plan on how not to get shot.

"You didn't know where to seat people at the restaurant. Mario noticed it, the wait staff noticed it, and so did I. It got us all wondering about you. And you spread lies to try to throw everyone off, like telling Mario you were going to meet someone at the house because you must have known that Catherine had a date planned with Charlie later that night. What you didn't know was that he never showed up, so the body was discovered before you had a chance to plant that bloody glove in his house, forcing you to leave it in his greenhouse and hope someone would find it there. And there was never anything wrong with your hair. You had it changed to match Catherine's, and wore that scarf to hide it until after you'd killed her, then you chopped it off and dyed it black. You told me that your sister made fun of your hair, but Ramona told me that her mother never saw it, because you didn't change it until the day after the murder. Your niece saw you with that scarf on your head the morning her mother was killed, and the next day you showed up with black hair, so Catherine couldn't possibly have seen it. But it was using my recipe that really gave you away."

Nicki slowly lowered her hands, keeping her gaze locked with Cynthia's. "I gave that recipe to the hostess at Mario's. The person who said she was Catherine Dunton. The only way for you to get that recipe is if you were impersonating your sister, so we'd all think she was still alive, at least until you thought Charlie was supposed to show up."

"She turned me down," Cynthia sneered. "It was my money too, and she turned me down. The auction house called. They had a rare book, in perfect condition and signed by the author, but the owner wouldn't let it go for less than ten thousand dollars. It would have been the crown jewel of my collection. But my sister refused to give me the money from the trust. 'It's too much,' she said. And how she was tired of her daughter and me always asking for money. How dare she put me in the same category as that brat of hers? I worked all my life. I'm not the one who pretended to go to school for years and years just so I could live off someone else's money." The gun waved back and forth as Cynthia's eyes glittered with rage. "It wasn't just *Catherine's* father who set up that trust for us. He was *my* father too, and half that money was mine. I shouldn't have had to beg for it."

Just then a loud crash came from somewhere downstairs. Cynthia's head whipped around at the same time the chief shouted, "Get down Nicki!"

Nicki dove for the ground, rolling until she was between the bed and the wall. With her head glued to the floor, all she could see was a shuffling of feet before she squeezed her eyes closed. If someone was going to shoot her, she didn't want to see it.

She yelped and flailed her arms when she was lifted up by the waist.

"Stop, Nicki! It's me."

Dropping her arms, Nicki looked up into the deep brown of

Matt's eyes. Without a word she threw her arms around his neck and buried her face in his chest. Matt's arms closed around her as her knees began to buckle.

"Okay, I've got you." His arms tightened a bit more. "Let's get you out of here. Everyone's waiting for you outside."

CHAPTER TWENTY-FIVE

IT WAS EARLY EVENING AS, BY AN UNSPOKEN AGREEMENT, everyone gathered in Nicki's kitchen. Jenna had made a stop at Eddie's Burger Diner on the way, having declared that none of the amateur detectives were doing any cooking, which was fine with Nicki.

As the crowd around her kitchen island grabbed the burger of their choice and dug into a mountain of fries, she stood contentedly next to Matt, laughing as the very health-conscious Dr. Alex took a big bite of a greasy cheeseburger, and Maxie picked up a French fry with a napkin before popping it into her mouth. Nicki lifted her glass of sparkling water just as Matt pushed a huge pile of fries in front of her, while he held a double-decker burger under her nose. Nicki wouldn't have been able to get her mouth around the thing, much less eat all of it. She rolled her eyes and pushed his hand away.

"I can't eat that." She squinted up at him. "Why are you always determined to shove food into me?"

"Why can't you make a meal of something more than a glass of sparkling water? You have to eat something."

"Matt." Nicki thought he was probably still reacting to what had happened in Catherine's house, but he really needed to find another way to deal with his anxieties. "I spent the entire afternoon doing cooking demonstrations. Good chefs always taste what they make. If I eat any more, I'll burst."

Matt glanced over at Ty. "That whole charity thing happened on your watch. Did she eat or not?"

"Like a horse," Ty responded, winking at Nicki when she glared at him.

"Just once I'd like to see that," Matt mumbled.

"Just once I'd like your girlfriend to stay out of trouble." Chief Turnlow nodded a greeting all around as he removed his hat and stepped into the kitchen. "I hope you don't mind me letting myself in."

"Grab a burger and tell us what's going on." Jenna bumped against Alex to make room for the chief at the island.

Deciding there was no use in even trying to set the chief straight anymore, Nicki ignored his girlfriend comment. She noticed that Matt did too. Telling herself it was no big deal, she smiled at the chief of police as he grabbed a burger. She wasn't going to dwell on the whole Matt-boyfriend thing when she was much more interested in what the chief had to say about Cynthia's arrest.

"Did you throw Cynthia into solitary confinement after she confessed?" Maxie demanded. "It's the least you could do after she held a gun on our Nicki."

Matt groaned. "Let's not talk about that part. I'm going to have nightmares for a year."

"Now who's being dramatic?" Nicki laughed, but she kept her gaze on the chief. "*Did* Cynthia confess?"

"She's on her way over to the Santa Rosa jail, and no, she didn't confess. She demanded a lawyer and clammed up." The chief shrugged. "I expected that. But it isn't going to help. I had heard enough while I was trying to get behind her in the house, and Danny called on my way back here from Santa Rosa. When my deputy searched her house, he found not only the recipe card you described in detail, and a pair of dark green pants hanging with a blue blouse, but he also found an entire Zelite knife set in the back of her bedroom closet. It was missing the chef's knife."

"My heavens, I guess Ramona was right when she said that her aunt never threw anything away." Maxie reached over and put her hand on her husband's arm. Mason gave it a reassuring pat.

"Is your deputy on his way to the forensics lab with that evidence?" the former police chief asked.

Chief Turnlow nodded. He took a bite of his burger and squirted ketchup on the fries Jenna had pushed in front of him

"So why are you here instead of grilling the murderer?" Jenna asked, giving the chief a slight shove in the side with her elbow. The big man didn't budge an inch as he ate another fry before using one of the paper towels scattered about the counter to wipe his fingers.

"Thanks. It's been a long day and I was hungry." He nodded at Nicki. "I'm here to give the official thank you and reprimand."

"Reprimand?" Maxie's indignant tone rang through the kitchen. "She kept an innocent man from being prosecuted by discovering the real killer. You should be giving her a medal, not a reprimand."

"Now, Maxie. Let the chief talk." Mason put an arm around his wife's shoulders and shook his head at her when she opened her mouth again.

Huffing out a sharp breath, Maxie shook her head right back at him. "I'm going to listen." She sent a glance over to Chief Turnlow. "And then I'm going to complain."

The chief laughed. "Fair enough." He leaned his hands on the counter. "Miss Connors. The City Council of Soldoff, and the members of the police department. would like to officially thank you for finding justice for one of our citizens.

Nicki grinned. "Chief Turnlow, the City Council of Soldoff, and especially the members of the police department, are very welcome." She made a wide gesture to include everyone around the kitchen island. "But it wasn't just me. Everyone here helped."

"By everyone, she means her little club of food and wine

groupies. But Nicki's the one who figured it out," Jenna declared. "And aside from the muffin, I haven't heard how." She raised one eyebrow at her friend. "Or was Cynthia Dunton's dastardly plan completely done in by a cranberry-orange muffin with raw sugar on the top?" She chuckled when Nicki blinked. "We've been hanging out for years. I know that turbinado is raw sugar."

"What else gave Cynthia away?" Like the chief, Maxie also leaned forward, clearly eager to hear the answer.

"Remember that night?" Nicki asked, addressing the chief. "When we were in the dining room and I said something wasn't right, but I didn't know what?"

The chief nodded. "I told you to let me know when you figured it out."

"It was the clothes. It didn't really register with me at the time, but Catherine's blouse wasn't quite the same shade of blue that I'd seen her wearing at the restaurant, and her pants weren't dark green. When Alex told me that the pair she'd seen in the forensics lab was black, I knew it was wrong, but got interrupted by Beatrice Riley before I had a chance to really think it through."

She paused while her fingers began to drum against the countertop. "And it was strange the way she was making sure everyone knew about her hair mishap. She even mentioned it to Beatrice. Most women wouldn't have shown up in public at all until they'd had a chance to fix whatever was wrong, or at least they wouldn't have kept calling attention to it. And Suzanne didn't know about it either. Don't you think that's something her best friend would have told her? It's the kind of thing best friends talk about. But the muffins were her real downfall. I knew the minute I tasted one that it wasn't the recipe of an amateur baker, and when Suzanne confirmed that Cynthia had made them, I realized that it really *was* my recipe, the one I'd given Catherine that night at the restaurant. The only explanation was that Cynthia had been masquerading as her twin."

"Which is why she was acting so wonky that night," Jenna said.

"She'd never been a hostess at Mario's, so she had no idea where to seat the customers or who the regulars were."

"That's right," Nicki agreed. "And she had no idea that Catherine had promised me a table by the window that afternoon at the Society meeting. And when I talked to Ramona, she confirmed that her mother never said she disliked her sister's hair because Catherine never saw it. Ramona said Cynthia didn't show up with that black, shaggy cut until after Catherine died. Which meant there probably was no hair disaster at all. She had simply made it up so no one would question why she was wearing a scarf over her head."

"To hide the fact she'd had her hair dyed and cut to match her sister's." Alex nodded. "She went to a lot of trouble for ten thousand dollars."

"People have killed for less," the chief commented. "But I got real curious about what book she thought was worth killing her sister for, so I made a call to that auction house you mentioned, Nicki."

Nicki's hazel eyes crinkled at the corners. "You did?"

Chief Turnlow nodded, a smile tugging on his mouth. "Yep. They confirmed that they'd contacted Cynthia Dunton about a private sale of a book by one of their clients, and Cynthia agreed to the purchase price of ten thousand dollars."

"What book did she want that badly?" Matt asked. "Did the auction house tell you?"

"Yes, they did." Now the smile grew until it covered the entire lower half of the chief's face. "It was a mint condition, first edition signed by the author." He curled his lips inward as his belly began to shake with silent laughter. "It was signed by Sir Arthur Conan Doyle, and was *The Hound of the Baskerville*s."

Matt stared at him for a moment, then burst into laughter. So did everyone else as Nicki put her hands on her hips.

"Oh sure. Now you know the name of a Sherlock Holmes book."

Once the laughter had died down, the chief's facial expression fell into more sober lines.

"Now young lady, it's about that reprimand for interfering in police business."

Nicki smiled, nodded and tuned him out. All her friends were here, rolling their eyes and shaking their heads at the chief's lecture on the proper behavior for a civilian.

And next to her was Matt. Her editor, her boss, and lately her sidekick. And maybe, just maybe, something more.

Nicki's smile grew wider. Good friends who were really family, and a future relationship with possibilities beyond a great friendship. Life didn't get any better than that.

READER'S CORNER

To My Readers:

Thank you for spending time to read *A Special Blend of Murder*. As you know, the book takes place in the wine country located in Northern California. Some of the best wines in the world are produced in the Sonoma and Napa Valley regions. In October of 2017, deadly fires broke out across the two valleys and up into the northern coastal region. Forty-two people lost their lives, and almost nine thousand homes and businesses burned to the ground. I live in Northern California, about forty miles southeast of our wonderful wine country, and know how resilient this State is in the face of disasters. But if you happen to be living or visiting near the San Francisco area, our wine country could really use your support. So please visit, if you get the chance. It's still beautiful country, and the vast majority of the wineries are open and always happy to have visitors. There are so many wonderful wineries and restaurants and places to stay, it would be nearly impossible to list them all. But I have to admit, I do have some favorites that I am happy to recommend in this and future books in the series. I'm sure Nicki and all her friends would give them a "thumbs up".

Sincerely,

Cat Chandler

I have no affiliation with these two eateries, which rank among my favorites. I simply enjoy visiting them.

THE SUNFLOWER CAFÉ

Located right on the square, this is a favorite, and busy, eatery in the town of Sonoma. It's always struck me as a step right back into the '60's, with a definite "hippie" kind of vibe and flare. It's breakfast that usually draws a good crowd here, and is a great choice if you want to get into town early and grab a bite near all the tasting rooms on, and just off, the square.

THE GIRL & THE FIG

A real crowd favorite, so you might have to wait for a long wait for a table if you don't make a reservation. Especially on a weekend. I don't recall if I've ever hear or read where the name came from, but they do sponsor a foundation called Funding Imaginable Goals—which kind of sounds like the acronym was made up to fit the name. This cute place, with a great bar and outdoor dining, has a French bend to it, although they do have a pretty good burger, which I'm sure did not originate in France. I'm partial to the Brussels sprout salad. They also have their own blend of wine, but I have to admit that I've never tasted it. If you do stop by there and give it a try, please drop me a line and let me know how it was.

AUTHOR'S NOTE:

I really do appreciate all my readers. Time is precious, and it means a lot that you would spend some of yours reading my book. If you'd like to follow more adventures of Nicki and her friends, please sign up for my reading list:

http://eepurl.com/dhGQYr

New subscribers will receive a link to download a file containing a full chapter that was not used in any of the books. This is a backstory about how Nicki, Jenna and Alex met in The Big Apple, New York City.

You'll be notified of new releases in my mystery series, and I never share email addresses with any other author or organization. What goes on my list, stays only on my list. I also do not inundate my subscribers with emails of weekly or even monthly newsletters. This is for new release announcements only, and occasionally (very occasionally) a notice of something coming up concerning my books. I will also be adding additional free scenes or short stories only to my list subscribers, with the link appearing in the email.

Also, if you enjoyed the book, please consider leaving a review on Amazon. Good reviews make an author's day, and writing is a lonely business. Hearing a word of praise every now and again really gives a lift to those of us hunched over a keyboard for a good part of our day. If you have any suggestions you think would help improve the book, or find typos or other errors, please feel free to contact me at: cathrynchandlerauthor@gmail.com. I'm also always open to story ideas. Or if there is a particular character you'd like to see more of, please let me know.

And as always—Happy Reading!

Cat

www.CathrynChandler.com

ALSO BY CAT CHANDLER

A Food & Wine Club Mystery:

A Special Blend of Murder (May 2017; rev Feb 2018)

Dinner, Drinks and Murder (Aug 2017; rev Feb 2018)

A Burger, Fries & Murder (March 2018)

74530473R00115

Made in the USA
Middletown, DE
26 May 2018